Not Her Nor Him

ROBERT BUCKEYE

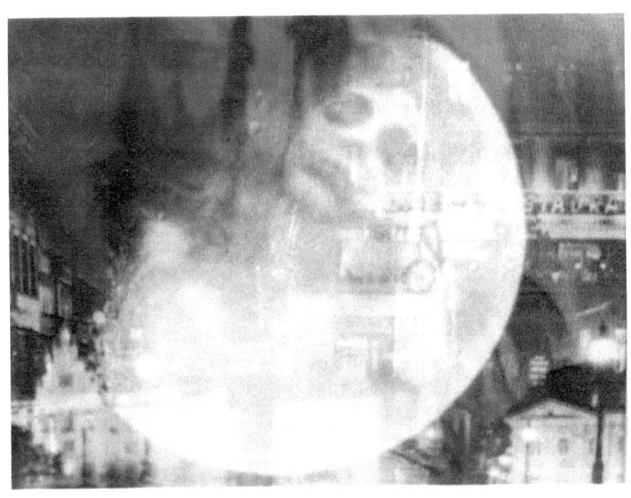

SPUYTEN DUYVIL
New York City

©2016 Robert Buckeye
ISBN 978-1-944682-22-4
Back cover image: Fred Cray
Front cover image: Jonathan Blake

Library of Congress Cataloging-in-Publication Data

Names: Buckeye, Robert, author.
Title: Not her nor him / Robert Buckeye.
Description: New York City : Spuyten Duyvil, [2016]
Identifiers: LCCN 2016022286 | ISBN 9781944682224
Classification: LCC PS3552.U336 A6 2017 | DDC 814/.6--dc23
LC record available at https://lccn.loc.gov/2016022286

for Ken Warren

S he sees him examine her. His eyes alert, attentive, large behind thick glasses. She knows what they think. What they always think.

She can no longer escape the not-knowing, but can't get her hands around it. As if in a dream, she sees him stop, walk back and forth, stare out the window. She sees him open his mouth, say something.

She doesn't understand the words. It is not father. Not his voice which is strong, clear, forceful. The man summoned by father to be him. Who called him forth.

Because. A recorded message.

You. A cough.

Him. His forehead wrinkles.

Her. A nod.

It is Berlin, 1931. She has a room in a pension near Alexanderplatz. One window looks out on the wall of a building opposite which forms four sides of a small courtyard. She keeps a small calendar on her table to count the days and mark them off, calculating weeks.

— — —

He waits. If he waits long enough. He writes something down in a notebook. The scratch of his pen against paper. If S. does not speak, he will ask her why she does not. In the spring we need to air out rooms. We need to breathe. He sights down his pen, a hint of a smile on his face. His nose is large and fleshy, his lips narrow and severe below a thick, dark moustache. Silence takes up space.

— — —

She holds silence in folded hands in her lap. It queues up in bread lines, waits for trams, looks for work. That one is a farmer. You can tell by his boots. His back bent by a lifetime of work. The one with thick glasses used to be a doctor. See his hand shake. He will not look you in the eye. That woman with the torn, silk dress is a mistress of a man big in the government. Look how other women shun her. In her eyes the desolation of those who have sacrificed themselves for love.

History does not have enough rooms for all the silence it contains.

— — —

Those who come to him may not say anything. They may lie. Tell him anything they think will please him. He examines something in his notebook, crosses out something he has written. They may. He leans back, pulls his vest down. Their fingers never lie. If it is not their fingers, it is their chin or eyes. They may rub hands together, cross their legs. What they cannot control. Something compulsive. He taps his pen against the palm of his hand, examines her. Their bodies run away from them to tell anyone, anyone they can find, did you see, did you see?

— — —

She sees herself as he sees her. As if she stands alongside him pointing out to him what she does. This woman sitting quietly in his office who knots and unknots a handkerchief, toys with a button on her blouse. As if she sits inside herself waiting for him to tell her what is next, what to say, what it means.

Hands know what is to be done. With glasses and forks it is easy, but whenever her hands do what they do without asking, her heart beats fast, nerves race, muscles tighten, eyes blur. Whenever her hand moves, she is startled by its action, as if it is not her hand and belongs to someone else. She always looks around to see if anyone has noticed. Hands don't lie but can be governed. Kept in sight.

She crosses her legs. Uncrosses them. As if he writes in his notebook, taps his pen, touches his nose in order to absorb her into him. The body in which she hides. The not-knowing never ignores what it does not know.

— — —

He has been a therapist ten years, more, read the literature, spoken to colleagues, gone to conferences, sat in at consultations. They tell him what he already knows, not what he needs to know. Case studies, graphs, charts. Distribution. Tendencies. No more than Rorschach blots we ask them to describe. Nothing they can explain or justify that one morning knocks when they least expect it, that one night, late, when they get up to pee is waiting for them.

S. might be the woman who was here this morning. The one yesterday. Their stories so much the same they get in the way of one another. He leans back, his eyes lidded. That describe patterns but not the one who sits in front of him.

— — —

He has seen her toy with a button on her blouse. Father's girl alongside him saw it. In the world of fathers, women are girls who must please. Every girl knows it even when she is a grandmother. The white-haired woman she saw down the street yesterday who unzipped the fly of a balding, stooped man and slipped her hand in. A tall, young man in khakis and blue work shirt smiling at a woman across the street and playing with the buckle of his belt. She leaned back against a building. Her hand dropped to her crotch. Two teenagers going by arm-in-arm. The girl's hand down the back of his trousers.

— — —

If S. says nothing
The nothing she fears yet embraces because she fears it less than
What she knows but will not give up, because if she does, brings it out into the open, airs it out, it will no longer be hers.

Her silence is not so much absence as its expression. As if S. must hold words in her hands, examine them, turn them over, to discover what they don't say in order not to say them. As if words disappear into themselves and can be understood only if they are other than they are. He looks out the window, examines a loose thread on his jacket. His pen taptapping against the desk.

—You make a virtue of silence. It can become a perversion.

— — —

A gooseneck lamp is the only light. He asks if she wants it on or off. Daylight may be sufficient. Or darkness may be. He does not say what.

She sees herself naked to the waist in the mirror. Her skin soft, breasts well developed, waist trim, hips rounded. Her face is ordinary. Her eyes are wide, lids pale lavender, eyebrows distinct. Her jaw is firm, cheeks fleshy. A nose like an axe. Her dark, thick hair is parted in the middle. She runs a finger across the slab of her brow. For a moment she touches a nipple.

Father says she is attractive. That she has become a woman. A real woman he says, the look on his face causing her to turn away. The one who has mysteriously moved in and taken up residence in her. Who has been there from the beginning.

— — —

He writes something down in the notebook. If he does not.

Memory is a double-edged sword. It keeps what it wants kept and buries what it wants buried. It does not forget what it wants forgotten and cannot find what it wants found. It is never there when it is needed and always there when it's not. To distinguish what happened from what was thought or imagined may be impossible and may not, in any case, help, but.

But is where it begins.

— — —

She would lie bent over on father's lap and when his hand came down, she raised her buttocks to meet it. She could not help herself. She wanted it. She. It was she.

Afterward she would touch herself, humiliated, not that she had been punished for having done something wrong, but because she needed to be punished before she could touch herself. There were days she would not make her bed or forget to run an errand.

She holds a hand up in front of her face.

Her hand.

His.

At night, in the deepest part of night, under heavy covers where no one can see or know anything, a hand steals down between her thighs. Whether she wants it to or not her finger starts to move, her wrist bends, her hand presses down, her dance begins.

The face in the mirror looks at her closely. The hand of the face in the mirror touches herself where his hand lingered.

— — —

—What you have.

For a moment he pauses. Last night Anne was silent at dinner. She always asked about his day, would tell him what the girls did, what she did. If she had been working in the garden. Who she had tea with. If she had any concerns, she would wait until the girls were excused.

—It is not a disease like cancer.

He examines something he has written down in his notebook. You're quiet she had said. Is there something the matter? At one moment she looked like she was going to say something more but thought better of it. She only looked at him until he had to look away.

—It is something we have inside us that never troubles us until it does. We all experience it from time to time. How can I describe it? When we are no longer at ease. When we are out-of-sorts.

—Call it a dis-ease.

He runs a finger over his moustache.

—When it persists.

For a moment he looks at her.

—Lasts.

— — —

Yesterday she saw a man plastering the wall of a church. He had the shoulders of a man she could love. His hair curled down the back of his neck the way father's does. She imagined going up to him, embracing him, his hand against the back of her head, his rough stubble against her cheek.

Father says she should find a man, marry. It's not right she wants to help him. She should have her own life. There comes a time, he says, his smile forced. When the bird must leave the nest. Abruptly he laughed. His hand on her shoulder meant to be reassuring. It's not that he does not love her. It's just. He looked across the room. His hand pressed down, pushed into her.

— — —

They think that they are no more than luggage that gets shunted from one place to another because it lacks a destination but continues to be shipped because luggage must go somewhere. On this trip they have chosen to make they know that there are regulations, rules, and laws that must be followed. Trains must run on time. Police make certain law is enforced. Schools turn out the good citizen. Inmates cannot run the asylum.

They fear they will be embarrassed by what he'll find. A whip? A dildo? He rubs his eyes. He's tired. Not so much fetishes as alternatives. You can't throw out the luggage and buy a new set.

—Do you get out much? See people?

— — —

He knows she sees him mornings. He may guess that afternoons she goes to cafes for tea. She is that kind of woman. He will not know that evenings she stands outside restaurants watching those who can afford dinners eat.

She goes to movies, lectures, and gallery openings, walks up and down streets, goes to the post office, shops, and if anyone says as much as hello to her, it is not her they greet. As if she looks like someone they know and they are, for a moment, confused. She needs someone to notice her, but no longer knows who they will notice if they do.

There are moments. All of a sudden, frightening moments, when she asks herself who she just talked to or where she had been.

She has lost her place, even if whatever place it had been she did not know she had lost it until it was no longer there. Whether she had lost it so long ago that it had never been there.

2

He sits behind her so that she cannot see him. He does so not to distract or disturb. He does not want to

For a moment he coughs, clears his throat. **The** he begins, but she does not hear the rest.

The **the** she must complete.

As if they are in a cinema. He will lean forward, look at her, ask himself what she's like. He knows why women come to the movies by themselves. It is always his story. She the no one never no one but always no one, a shadow of, misplaced, unheard.

She sees father raise a hand in a fist as if in a newsreel and the crowd roars. He sweeps a hand across his chest to take them in, the city they live in, the world. They nod to one another, lean forward to hear better. He stops to wipe his brow. Listen to him their look says. He's got it right. For a moment back-breaking days are forgotten, empty stomachs ignored.

She is no more than anyone else who has come to hear her father, but she is the only daughter whose father they have come to hear. He does not speak to the crowd mother said. He picks out one person to address. You cannot convince a crowd that you speak to them unless it feels you are speaking directly to each one of them and no one else.

She is the one in the crowd father picks out. When he speaks, she answers. As if she is two years old again standing outside his study listening to him. She hears him begin his speech, stop, walk back and forth, sit back down at his desk, his pen scratch against paper.

His smile under a thick, black moustache is infectious. His eyes shine behind thick glasses. His hair is full, unruly. He laughs and she laughs with him. He smiles and she smiles back. She rocks back and forth on her heels, shifts from one foot to another.

She keeps a photo that had been taken of them when she was a girl on the night table next to her bed. The thatch of his hair is dark, abundant, his forehead broad. His eyes are intense under rimless glasses, burning. His thick moustache is trimmed carefully, lips firm. He wears a suit, a white shirt with a stiff, high collar that tucks in under his chin, a cardinal red tie. She is calm, happy, her hair parted in the middle, her cheeks full, fleshy. Her dress is dark blue, buttoned to the neck, pleated A white vee pattern on the dress just above her breast forms a triangle with her shoulders, framing her face.

— — —

—What are you

For a moment he pauses. Something Anne said last night. She is an only child and as much as her father loved her he missed having a son. At moments she saw him turn away from her so that she would not see the disappointment on his face.

—Thinking?

He is the youngest son. When he was still a child the legacy of the heir had already been played out. Thomas would take over the shop when father stepped down. Franz left. He had gone to Paris and no one had heard from him. He wanted to be an artist, but had never succeeded at anything he did.

—What word comes to mind when I say thinking?

— — —

As if she knows what he will ask and hears him before he speaks. What she must dig up, unearth, bring to the surface, so that everyone can see it, acknowledge its life. The words he speaks to call forth hers. For her to answer his question she must play his game.

It does not have to do with the mind, but with what the mind does not know. For a moment she thinks of turning around to look at him but does not. The one who will tap her on the shoulder say, say, say. As if she faces a prosecutor in court who won't let her go until he is satisfied she tells him what he wants to hear.

She has seen so many of them before. In a hospital. Where had it been? When? She remembers she turned away and examined a white stucco wall. The doctor waited. She never says anything but they always wait for her to speak. In her lap her hands ball themselves into fists.

— — —

—What comes to mind when I say the word crowd?

A son would carry on his name, but Anne would be at risk. The last girl had been so difficult for her to bear she almost lost it. If she became pregnant again, the doctor said, shaking his head.

She knows young, attractive female patients may attach themselves to him. Already their two daughters compete with her for his affection. A son will give her the attention, affection and love his daughters give him.

The boy wants to be like father. The son resents mother being taken from him. The man replaces father, though he never does. Always the son who can never be his own father. Every day they come to see him

When we love we are no longer who we are but someone else in a story we have not written.

— — —

13

As if he has moved closer, seated himself directly behind her, leaned over her shoulder, whispered in her ear. His breath slow, calm, an in-and-out that brushes against her cheek. She waits for a hand to reach across the back of the chair.

His hand.

The one that

She sees them sitting alongside one another in a theatre. On the screen handsome men lean over to kiss beautiful women sitting on couches, looking out windows, waiting in beds. Bearded men draw pistols to shoot, swords to strike. Active men mount horses, drive cars, fly, race away, toward. Dark men raise their hands to challenge, hit, defeat. Everyone follows what happens on the screen, their breath deepening, anxious, worried, their pulse rapid, while their hands reach for hands, caress thighs, touch breasts, themselves.

He turns to her, points them out on the screen. She sees them sitting alongside one another on the patient's couch. In a moment she sees herself touch him outside his trousers. Frantically she unbuttons his trousers and pulls them down, runs her hand over his erect shaft. In a moment he pushes her down and she takes him in her mouth. With a hand he moves her head back and forth. A groan escapes him. She begins to gag.

She does not look up. She cannot see his face. She does not want to see his face. The direction in which she is now compelled to look is towards the spot where he himself is located.

— — —

Women follow their men. You see them on their way to market, the butcher, baker. Children trail after them, ride piggyback on their mother's backs. Women who no longer follow their men protect what they have between their legs.

What they have given away has cost them. Women who follow their men but are not happy give away what they have. Their gift has been no gift, but one man's trash is another's treasure. Women who no longer have any men know that age has made what they have irrelevant. What had been the point?

—What word do you think of when I say obey?

— — —

The screen is dark. As if her hand moved across her face to cover her eyes. She crosses her legs, abruptly swings one leg forward, back. The theater will fill up. Everyone will be here to see who she is. They know what she does, have known it for a long time, but they must hear her say it. Those who will challenge what she says, ask why she remains silent. Those who have come to gloat, jeer, laugh. Who drag along

Father to make sure she has got it right. Mother who worries about her. It is not easy to be daddy's girl, she says, an ironic smile smeared across her face. You must not disturb father, she says. He has to write his speech. You must not bother him, she says. He has to read the papers. Leave him alone, she says. He needs rest.

The drunken couple in the next apartment. As soon as the day begins the vodka bottle is out. By evening their day is a lost cause and the only recourse is more vodka. They focus bloodshot eyes with difficulty, but they always manage to see her. What are you looking at? Their voices contemptuous. You think you're better than us?

For months she writes father saying she must join him. She can no longer live in Russia. She can help. She will do. He knows. If not one thing, then another. She can. Berlin is a mistake. Wrong.

The words unfold, slide up, float unheard, come down, stand in line, written with a pencil on a small piece of paper.

— — —

When S. clenches her hands into a fist. When her hands are at rest between her thighs. When she raises a hand as if to protect herself. When she runs a hand down a thigh. When she sweeps a hand back and forth.

She cannot stop the incessant movement of her hands no matter how much she makes the effort. She means for him to see them. She hides what they say, but will have put them in a place she wants him to discover.

—Hands. What word comes to mind when I say hands?

— — —

As if he has come back to his seat after going to the restroom or gone out for a smoke. A surgeon in a white coat about to make an incision. He will wash his hands, pull on plastic gloves. He will rearrange instruments on a table, check the IV, say something to the nurse. For a moment he will touch the skin where he'll cut.

It is lungs. Someone's back. Goiters. Stomach. Uterine issues. Whatever they say it is the same disease. Life. Her fingers pull at the fabric of her dress. What was it? She can't remember.

Before the surgeon begins he will tell her that if he does this, does that, chances are good that everything will be all right. Nevertheless we must take into account that something unexpected might happen. Chances are slight. But. Things happen. She should know the possibilities. What her options are.

She knows she must empty herself. Evacuate everything

before he can operate. Yesterday she retrieved shit from the toilet bowl and smeared it across the bathroom mirror. She does not know why. The face in the mirror is never hers, but she sees in it something she has not seen before. Something that will not, must not be broken.

— — —

She says nothing because when she speaks they do not hear. They hear only want they want to hear, understand what is already understood. Their words never more than chits in the game they play.

If she does not talk that does not mean she does not speak. Everyone finds a way to say what she has to say, however she can say it. It may be a nervous twitch, a cough, a sudden movement.

S. bites her lip, does not meet his glance, breathes with difficulty.

—What word comes to mind when I say talk?

— — —

Stalk she thinks. Stalk. To see what is not to be seen without being seen.

The legless veteran propped against a building, his hand out. The drunken storm troopers staggering down streets, singing the *Horst Wessel Lied*, sweeping away everything in their path. The woman in front of a grocer, asking for credit to a man who cannot afford to give any for fear he will be standing in her place tomorrow.

Curtains move in windows. Heartbeats slow. They heat hot water for tea or take a slug of vodka. They have seen nothing. They never see anything. It was not them. Tonight it was not them.

Yesterday she saw a woman in a royal blue, floor-length dress and scarlet cloche hat approach a man in a black bowler, a mud-brown topcoat over a houndstooth check suit, an account book sticking out of the pocket of his topcoat. For a moment he looked her up and down, taking his time, before he pulled her dress open. He cupped a breast in one hand, pulled at the nipple. His nose was red, bulbous, his lips thick. His other hand opened and closed into a fist. The woman looked over his shoulders. Her eyes vacant, blank.

She waits for the screams to subside. She never knows whether they are hers or ones she hears in the next room, down the street. Sometimes she thinks

She can no longer remember what it was.

3

He walks behind her, his footsteps moving away, stopping, beginning again, coming closer, hesitating, retreating, as if they have a life their own, one that. Never anything less than

....

An aimlessness in search of itself that calls attention to itself as much as her silence does. What is meant to be heard but not spoken. Listened to, not said.

She sees him notice her finger her blouse. He does not miss how her hands drop to her lap, how she clasps them together so tightly her knuckles are white. In the attention of the clinician she sees the recognition of the man. The not-knowing never forgets what it should not forget.

At the far end of the room when he turns around in his walk, he can see her face in profile. A firm jaw, fleshy cheeks, blunt nose, lips slightly open, as if something has surprised her, long dark hair in a pigtail, the nape of her neck.

She can only lose herself in herself.

— — —

Her silence a stone wall, a refuge, an answer. It shifts control, sets the agenda, defines the terms.

A refusal to play the game, if not a fear he will rig it.

A distrust, if not dismissal of the therapeutic.

A decision to ignore if not circumvent the rules we live by.

A way to delay what happens.

She listens to what silence tells her, not the speech that follows silence. She knows that when she speaks she can no longer be who she is, that speech prevents her from

Something that cannot be said. S. knows it cannot, should not be said, but does not know what it is. Something only silence can tell her.

Its endlessness.
Always, but not yet.

— — —

Father puts jazz on, dances to it, in order to understand the relation of jazz to the industrial world. Its syncopation, he says — its endless repetition — does nothing more than replicate the machine in the factory. But. He pauses, runs a hand across his forehead. At moments. He sweeps a hand back and forth in front of him. Like drums in the jungle.

Berlin is singing she wants to tell him. Voices hoarse with drunkenness and hunger. No one sings on an empty stomach but they have not seen Berlin. A sound like no other. A beat that is a pulse. That leaps out from alleys, seizes you, puts its hands around your throat. That cry out they are not heard.

Yesterday she saw storm troopers repeatedly bash the head of a man against the side of a building. They had to hold him up to demand his identification papers, ask him questions, but he had nothing to say, even after they slapped him across the face a few times. His face was bloodied. There was an ugly bruise on his forehead and a gap in his mouth where teeth had been. Sing something for us, they said. Sing.

— — —

Father has prepared S. to be the woman he needs who may not be her as much as the woman he has seen from the beginning. His anima. The she who is everything.

His decision to send S. to him may not be to bring her back to him as much as it is to keep her from underfoot. She is not the daughter he wants, even if no daughter can be. Her decision to undergo analysis may be her effort to be the woman he wants her to be, even if she already knows she never can be. If she understands herself in ways she does not now, she will no longer see father the same way. She will be even less the woman he wants her to be.

Father should be here. If he saw them together, even if S. defers to him, lets him speak for her, he would see....

Father is here, even when he is not. S. lives in a world of fathers and if she cannot be with father she will find another man to be father. She will find fathers wherever she can. The shadow that shadows her.

The sound of his steps in the room tracking her.

— — —

When she saw him, she thought, at first, it was him. Go up to him, she told herself, embrace him, feel his hand against the back of your head, his rough stubble against your cheek.

At first, he seemed puzzled. His brow furrowed and he examined her closely. Then he smiled, put an arm around her. I'll be finished in half an hour, he says. Where can I find you? It was not him, but she told him.

She apologizes for her room. It is small and she has not been able to do anything about cockroaches. They are everywhere. She has to brush them off pots and pans, books, clothing. They invade her dreams, crawl over her body, seek out her nostrils, her mouth.

Don't, he says, putting a hand against her cheek. They don't want us to live. His lips brush hers. We take what they can't take from us. His hand touches her breast.

What happened happened as it happens. The moment he. When she. Her nipples harden at the memory.

— — —

When S. fingers her blouse, clasps her hands tightly together, folds them in her lap, brushes a lock of hair off her forehead, briefly touches herself when she thinks he will not notice.

When she stretched a hand out in front of her and closed it into a fist before opening it.

When he asked her what word she associated with obey, she exhibited a state of marked sexual excitement.

When he asked her what word she associated with talk, she only looked at him, her eyes apprehensive, uncertain. A moment later she smiled before quickly covering her mouth with a hand.

Puppets in a theater.

Who — what — holds the strings, pulls them?

It may not be as much who or what as why. He needs to find the who that calls forth the what that will cause the why to speak.

Are her hands the only hands here? Do they speak to him, father, herself? Does someone else speak for them? The details pile up as S. begins to fade.

— — —

The day father is not at breakfast she goes to his study, but he is not there. He must not be up yet. She goes to his bedroom and sees him lying under the covers. He is always up by the time she wakes. Every day she comes into the kitchen and sees him sipping *chai*. Every day she sees him read on the porch or in his study bent over his desk writing.

It is no more than a stuffed gray cloth head with a black wig that has slipped down in father's bed, its eyes hard shell military buttons, the moustache a strip of black cloth pasted on, the mouth a slit cut in the fabric. For a moment she puts a finger into the slit that is its mouth and feels goose feathers.

He'll be back, mother says. He had to go and did not want to worry you. When you are older, you'll understand. He'll be back tonight. If not tonight, the next night. Her eyes are gentle when she brings her to her breast, but her chin is set, firm.

The stuffed gray cloth head slips into her bed after the lights go out. It pulls her to him and squeezes her tightly. Goose feathers spill onto her hair. Its black metal button eyes glitter. One or two goose feathers have spilled out of the slit which is its mouth. Kiss me, it says.

Years have passed, but it was this morning.

4

She sees father at his desk and if words do not come to him, he pauses, looks out the window, gets up, goes over to it, looks out. When he becomes aware she that she come into the study, he turns from the window, smiles, gestures for her to join him. It was sunny she remembers, the sky cobalt blue, the sun a pale gold wafer.

She sees herself press her forehead against the window pane, her jaw set, a stray curl pasted against her forehead. The surface of the glass is rough, ridged, pock-marked with bubbles, scored with scratches. The window pane vapors with her breath. The ice cold glass against her skin causes a sudden, sharp splitting pain across her forehead.

He goes to the window, he says. He goes to the window to see what he cannot see from his desk.

— — —

S. has chosen silence less than it has chosen her. She questions him more urgently by it than by anything she can say. The voice that speaks through hers that of a stranger.

YES, NOW, AT LAST.

So much babble.

The stupid formalities we must honor. The empty words speak, even if it is YES, NOW, AT LAST we want.

S. knows her silence is wrong, a colleague says. It is obstinate, defiant. As a girl she learned children should be seen not heard. As a woman she knows that she should speak only when asked.

If she does not. If she says nothing when asked to speak, it is as perverse as saying what she wants to say when she feels like saying it. She holds on to it not as if it's an obligation. A trust.

One speaks as one can. As one must. Language may be ours insofar it does not belong to us.

— — —

Brown shirts plowing into a crowd of demonstrators outside a bakery, truncheons swinging back and forth, everything rushing around her, a rapidly turning kaleidoscope she can neither escape nor stop. She is knocked down, her purse lost, finds herself sobbing against a wall, brown shirts and demonstrators gone, blood on the street.

The sudden silence was deafening. Overhead a flight of grackles flew by. A sparrow warbled as if it were a day like any other. She waited, not able to move, listening for the sound of steps, voices talking, store door bells tinkling, wagons rattling down the street to tell her life had resumed.

Every day she hears cries on the streets of Berlin and every night they follow her to her room. The old couple down the hall who get at one another all day. The woman who takes men to her room late at night.

— — —

—We sit across from one another. You say nothing.

For a moment he examines something on his desk, looks out the window, leans back in his chair. He runs a hand across his forehead. What S. knows without knowing it does not have to be said. What he expects her to say she will not say.

—Who do we tell what we will not tell anyone else? We trust family, friends, loved ones, but we do not want them to know everything about us, even if we can hide nothing from them.

He gestures with a hand, at what, why he does not know, as if it were some reflex.

—Sometimes it is easier to talk to a stranger. One who sits next to us on the tram or stands in line behind us at the post office. We trust them because we will never see them again. They cannot betray us.

—It is more difficult with priests or doctors. We expect them to keep the knowledge they have of us safe. We give them our trust because every time we see them they know things about us no one else does. If we do not, we cannot tell them anything.

— — —

For weeks now every day has been the same day. A leaden-gray sky, cruel winds, biting cold. When she waits for a tram, she tucks her chin down into her cloth coat, pulls up its collar, wind lashing against her face. Her gloves are threadbare, fingers numb. She waits for spring but spring does not come.

What mattered, her situation, call it what you will, did not matter. She comes to his office as she must. She leaves as she must. Thomas — doubting Thomas everyone calls him — will be waiting for her. Every afternoon he is there. There seems to be nothing wrong with him and he never causes any difficulty. He's harmless everyone says. A big man who lurches when he walks, as if his body is a bag of groceries which shifts with every step. He always makes the sign of the cross in front of her.

You know why they call me Thomas? he asks. You must know the Bible. All you Jews do. One eye wanders. He hitches up white hospital-grade pants which have slipped down his ample stomach. His belly button is red, raw, as if he picks at it. When the police came for my father, I told them I did not know him. I had never seen him before. He snuffles.

They hear you in the night, he says. The neighbors tell me. Father, you cry. Father. His pale blue eyes grow moist and for a moment he rubs them.

— — —

S.s' hands are marked by prominent pale blue veins and several birthmarks. Her skin is stretched tightly across them. Lines crisscross back and forth. What he understands about patients at moments seems less useful than what a medium sees when she examines hands. They see paths. He has only questions.

Slight hands, frail. A doll's hands. If he takes her hands, presses them against his.

Women let doctors see their bodies, touch them in a way they would not permit other men to do. No longer men but priests immune to the desires of the flesh. The money patients pay a contract that guarantees the doctor's integrity. No longer a man but a prostitute paid for his detachment.

If we place our hands on them, how is it not our hands that feel what they feel when they are our hands?

— — —

She sees a man kissing her and she says, no. He touches her breast, and she says, no. They are standing and then they are sitting. She says, no, as though she has lost something, says no, as if she needs to hear it again, convince herself that she means it, but as much as his fingers seek her out, her body answers back.

They are standing and then they are sitting. Her dress is above her waist and has been unzipped in the back. He does not say love but his touch is a comfort, benediction, but she says no, even if her body wants what her no denies.

She cannot see his eyes. His face is blank. She reaches out to touch his face, caress it, but as much as she wants to see who it is she does not want to know. She is afraid he'll leave and not come back as much as she fears he will stay.

— — —

She follows his gestures more closely than his words. At one moment she closed her eyes and crossed her legs when he had done something with his hand, some gesture he does not remember, as if it had been a command, an order. When he paused to examine his pen, she ran a hand over a thigh, the hint of a smile flickering on her lips.

Whenever she sees it, she must….

Whatever must tells her.

There are moments he feels she remains silent in order to provoke him. That she wants him to raise his hand in anger at her refusal to speak. If he struck her, she would see that he was a man, no longer a doctor, and she a woman, not a case for him to evaluate, resolve, file.

He needs to be detached, clinical, but it is a cardinal rule of his that the analyst must possess the freedom the patient has to acquire.

If he put his hand on her shoulder, said. It does not matter what he would say. Her shoulder will be soft, yielding. His hand will do what hands do.

5

This morning when she washed herself she stopped to examine herself in the mirror. Her skin is dark, that of a gypsy, hips full, breasts well-developed, nipples rust-brown, prominent. She smiled. She likes her body, even if her face is ordinary, her nose an affront, forehead a ship's prow, pronounced, blunt. Burning black eyes eyed her. For a moment she cupped a breast in a hand.

She thought she had drawn the curtains across the bathroom window but at one moment saw she had left a gap in the curtains. She always felt uneasy when anyone looked at her, but the thought that someone might see her when she was not aware that he did pleased her. She wet a finger with her lips and rubbed a nipple back and forth. Something stirred in her.

She wanted the right man to see her, but could not bear it if he did. He would think that she displayed herself because she was available, could be had. She remembered his hand on her shoulder at the end of last session.

In the window of an apartment across the alley she saw a man looking at her. For a moment she was confused as if she thought touching her breast had caused him to materialize. She shut her eyes. She was not only embarrassed, nervous but also, in a way that surprised her, aroused. She felt an urge to turn her back, slip her skirt down, bare herself to him. When she touches herself at night, desire overwhelms her, as if there is nothing she will not do, nothing at all, to satisfy herself. The dark night into which she sinks that humiliates her but which she must have.

For a moment she steadied herself against the edge of the sink before she went over to the window, one hand covering her breasts, to pull the shade across. She saw his glance transfixed, frozen. She smiled. He may have thought she would be his, but she controlled him. The devil whispered to her, but she ignored him.

— — —

S.'s fingers coil around one another like snakes in a pit. Her eyes withdrawn into her head, her mouth open, skin stretched tightly across her forehead. In a moment she smiles at him, as if it is a game.

Last night his older daughter took his hand while she sat in his lap. Look, Mommy, she said, holding his hand in hers. Anne, who had been crocheting, looked up, affectionately smiled.

Children amuse us when they do what they do because we feel that they do not know what they are doing, but they do, even if they may not able to say why. The daughter must compete with mother for father.

She took one of his fingers and for a moment put it into her mouth. Two children playing games, Anne said, smiling, but her cheeks reddened.

There is a but.

A but that lives us.

— — —

For a moment she had been startled. If she had slipped her skirt down, gestured to the man, but if she had, it surprises her, she would not be afraid. Whether he was real or not she had brought him to the window.

She imagined him turn away from the window, leave his apartment, descend in the lift, walk slowly but confidently across the courtyard, pause for a moment to look up at her window before he entered her building, walked up the stairs.

His steps deliberate, certain. He would not knock. He would know she was waiting for him.

She glanced at herself in the mirror. Full breasts, nipples erect, mouth open, lips wet. Burning black eyes triumphant, if not evil. A look she had not recognized before. In a moment she was exhausted and leaned against the sink.

She felt herself blushing deeply. Once she knew he was there she had for a moment loosened the belt that keeps her in check, thrown away the leash that lashes her every day.

—   —   —

—Lean back. Rest. Your mind is clear. Do you see a landscape? Yes?

He places his hands on either side of her head, as if to cradle it.

—You are walking through a field. The grain is tall, blown by a soft wind and crests like waves swelling gently in the ocean. You stop to pick some flowers at the edge of the field. Vetch, Queen Anne's lace, chicory. You smell their fragrance. Overhead a hawk floats. A bird calls out and is answered.

—The sky is blue, except for several small motionless clouds. The sun bright, warm. For a moment you stop to shade your eyes. The field at the edge of the hill near the horizon shimmers from the heat of the day.

—When I tell you to close your eyes, you will enter a world that is familiar, one that you know, but one that, nevertheless, seems mysterious. You will describe it to me. When I clap my hands you will wake and not remember where you've been.

—   —   —

She is at a sidewalk café down the street. She puts a cube of sugar in her tea and stirs it. She hears Strauss on the radio, laughter, sees someone at the next table put an arm around a loved one. The waiters are polite, respectful.

This woman who stops afternoons at the cafe, goes home afterward, cooks dinner for herself, reads or goes to the movies, goes to sleep and sleeps the night through without tossing and turning is a woman she had known once. Every now and then she thinks about her, as one thinks about someone one knew in school and has just seen a photo of her in the yearbook.

The soporific sound of Strauss, laughter. She runs a finger around the lip of the tea cup, intent on the inexorable advance of her finger. She is a stranger. Not that she is a foreigner. Everwhere she is she is a stranger.

Every day she must, should, but can't, won't. If she could, did, must would become can, should will, but if she did whatever must or should wants it would not be who she is.

The waiter asks if she wants anything more. For a moment she looks up at him. He has a beak nose, dark black hair slicked back, hollow cheeks, dark shadows under his eyes. She wants to say something, anything, begin a conversation, but no, she says. Nothing. She balls her napkin up.

She knows what is best for her, wants to remain the way she is, knows if she does she can keep everyone at bay. She feels that it is time for her to change, do whatever is demanded of her, but life, she knows, cannot be lived as it is lived. She needs what she cannot let go.

Every night after she turns the lights off, pulls the covers back, gets into bed and closes her eyes, she finds herself in the Sahara Desert. She sees riders on the horizon, but they do not notice her. For weeks she follows them but keeps her distance. They live in a world she does not understand and would not, in any event, accept her, it's just

To see them. Know that they are there.

— — —

He sees S. wait for a streetcar after she leaves, her eyes lidded, dark shadows under them, face drawn, strained, shoulders bent. She looks down the street to see if it is approaching, the look on her face desolate, as if the streetcar will take her not to Alexanderplatz but to the future already seen everyday on the streets of Berlin.

What he does is a benign, homeopathic version of the violence S. sees everyday. Berlin's brown shirts and bankers, maimed veterans and starving poor, prostitutes and society women. He gives patients small doses of it so that they are better able to absorb the larger doses inflicted on them everyday.

At moments they understand the violence they do themselves cannot compare to the violence the world does them. At moments they know there is no greater violence than what they do to themselves. At moments they don't care. They look at him as if he is in the way.

S. must return to what first turned her, even if it is no longer there, even if it was never there in the first place. What she knows, even if she cannot say why, she must put behind her before she can enter a future the past keeps her from approaching. He claps his hands together.

—You will wake.

— — —

The last night she sat with her sister, Nina, the evening she died, she could not forget the terrible fear in her eyes. For weeks Nina knew the end was near and bore up bravely. She held her hand and when Nina threw up wiped vomit from her lips. She applied a cold cloth to her brow, brushed hair off her forehead. Nina suffered in silence. She said nothing.

There was nothing to be done. She cried because she could do nothing and would miss Nina horribly.

Just before midnight, Nina's eyes suddenly widened and she seemed to recoil from what she saw. Nina was no longer aware she was at her side. Wherever she was it was no longer in this room. Whatever Nina saw she had no doubt it was death, final, irrevocable, and no fear could contain it.

Father loved Nina and when she was gone there was nothing she could do to replace her no matter how she tried. Those who lose a breast or leg can't let them go. They rub the scar, touch the stump, but what is gone does not come back, even if they can never let go of it.

—There are streets we cannot cross. Buildings we cannot enter.

As if she is speaking to herself. For a moment she glances at her hands folded in her lap.

—People we cannot meet.

She looks looks blankly at him, as if what she has said was no more than obvious, did not need to be said, but must, at certain moments, be said. The obvious is only obvious when it is not.

She did, had, speak, spoken.

— — —

It seems as if

He does not know why. As if when she spoke she became the therapist and he the patient. For weeks her silence had been that of the therapist whose silence forces a patient to say something, but when she spoke.

S. looks at him, as if she is him looking at her. It was uncanny. She a Jew, from the dusky steppes of the East. He a Christian, bourgeois to the core, a philistine.

He wants to take her hand and stroke it but only gestures vaguely in front of him.

— — —

She does not trust what her eyes tell her, but. She does not know how to say it. At first her silence got in the way, but once he began to listen to it, pay attention, examine it, hold it in his hands.

She could not have said anything if he had not opened his hands to her silence, so that she might place her words in them. Not what the words meant, but what the saying of them said.

At first she did not see it. She thought it was something else. It made no sense. Then she saw that it did. For her to surrender to him he had to surrender to her.

She sees a tiny sparrow on the branches of an elm outside the window. Its breast stippled, a white stripe through its crown, its eye stripe a bright orange. It flicks it tail and its beak moves as it calls out. For a moment it ruffles its feathers with its beak, the luster of its eye fading before it drops from sight.

6

On her way to therapy she had seen a streetcar come down the street. A paper and rag man wheeled his cart to the other side of the street. Two housewives eyed him and one said something to the other. The other shook her head. At the corner, a policeman had stopped to talk to the tobacconist.

An older man in a hospital-white gown crutched slowly ahead. Alongside him, a red-faced spastic jerked back and forth. Behind them a nurse carried bags. The hospital has been shut down, the halt and lame turned out to prowl the streets of Berlin, punching their fists in despair, in search of anyone who can spare a scrap of bread or cup of water.

Suddenly a plane flying low over a building down the street dropped leaflets onto the street and at one point she found herself among a group of them fluttering down, as happens in winter when a snow-squall suddenly springs up. She stopped to pick one of them up. **HITLER GIVES WORK, HITLER GIVES BREAD** it read. Down the street she saw a hotel porter sweeping the leaflets off the pavement into the gutter and when she reached the hotel, she dropped hers in the gutter.

There were swastikas chalked on sides of buildings. At street corners rifles were stacked neatly. Suddenly she felt Thomas alongside her. Do you see? he asked, but when she turned to answer he was not there. In the space where he had been she heard him say, The streetcar's come for us. It's not good.

— — —

—Why are you here? When I stopped to buy tickets for the opera, a policeman stopped me. What was I doing? he asked.

What the papers say may be exaggerated. The family maid always stretched things. He sees the poor begging but he has always seen them. But when the policeman stopped him at the opera house this morning, inexplicably he was afraid, as if down some dark street a hand had been placed on his shoulder.

—You must be careful.

Something is said to someone who says something to someone else who says something to someone who picks up the phone. Someone else is not at work, no one answers his door, no one sees him anymore.

—I'll write your father.

They will let them sweep everything away as long as they are not swept away, but once a broom sweeps it does not stop.

It was not until S. became his patient that the disturbing events in Berlin seemed to grow more frequent. It was not until she came to him that Anne asked questions about his work. It was not until she sat in front of him that he saw her when he looked at Anne.

— — —

His desk is large, four feet or so wide, close to three feet deep, its wood inlaid mahogany. On it there are a notebook, a calendar, a photo of his wife and his daughters, a glass paper weight, a brass paper slicer, a small bronze sculpture of Apollo, one of Plato.

She sees father at his desk, head bent over his writing. At moments he leaned back, looked at what he had written, crossed out a word, changed another, stopped, looked out the window, ran a hand across his forehead, took his glasses off, cleaned them.

Men at desks. Father kept a copy of Marx close by. He keeps Freud on a bookshelf behind the desk. At play at what plays them.

The weeks she said nothing because she did not know what to say, did not trust him nor herself to say anything, she began to see, not at first, she would not have believed it, that as he struggled with her silence it had become a desk she sat behind.

She wants to get up and sit on his desk, put her hand on it, say

It does not matter what she would say.

—No.

Her tone abrupt, sudden, harsh. Father sent her to Berlin. He had. She would not.

She hears some sound, as if it were blood pumping through her body that she can only hear when father is there.

— — —

The way S. looks at his desk, as if everything he had placed on it had been put there to keep her under his thumb. The questions he asked, the words he asked her to associate, the day he sat behind her so she would not see him seemed to her no more than obstacles he placed in front of her to block her way. The day he walked back and forth behind her to shatter the silence she had wrapped around herself.

—Its time is not our time, pointing to his calendar on the desk, but in the morning it sets the breakfast table, sends us out the door to work, to shop, plans when lunch or dinner will be, how the evening plays out.

Her black eyes burning, lips parted slightly. For a moment she runs a hand through her hair. After the second session she stopped braiding her hair in pigtails. He had noted it, but not given it any attention.

—Our time is never more than a whisper. We hear it everywhere, but as much as we search for it.

He waves a hand around the room. Why should we deny them? Gross asks. Transference happens. He laughed. Why should we deny ourselves? Don't be such a philistine. We must give ourselves the same freedom we give our patients.

—It eludes us.

As if he had not paused long enough that S. looked at him to see why he stopped.

—Even if we never cease hearing it.

— — —

This morning when she looked at herself in the mirror she saw that the blue-gray woolen scarf she had put on suited her well. Mother used to wrap a scarf around her neck to keep her from catching cold. When she saw herself in the mirror the feeling that she was being taken care of as mother had taken care of her had come back.

She pushes the chair back, stands, puts a hand down on the desk to steady herself, but when she notices her hand on his desk, she removes it quickly, as if she has done something she should not have done.

The hand she sees in front of her whose action it seeks is no more than its own shadow. For a moment she shakes her head back and forth as if to say no before she straightens, steps back. Suddenly she smiles.

It may have been a child who took her hand away from the desk, but it was a woman who put it there. Everyday she sees women on the streets of Berlin. There is no work and men lie in bed or go to the pub. Women use what God has given them to put bread on the table. Did not Eve offer Adam an apple?

She does not know how to go about it, what will happen, where it will lead, but she is overcome by feelings that are new, strange, but at the same time old, well-known, familiar.

The morning she was dressing in the bathroom and saw a man in the apartment across the courtyard staring at her. For a moment she looks at him. His eyes are more blue than she thought. Mist-blue, sea blue.

How is she to find her way back to life if the dream never ceases to invite her to join the dance?

— — —

When he got home last night Anne asked whether he had brought the coffee and sugar. He had forgotten. He was sorry. It had been. Is something the matter? she asked. For a moment she looked at him. I've trusted you to be discreet. You will not ruin what we have. Am I clear?

He did not know what to say. She knows transference with patients is possible, but it was not that, even if what it was, if it was anything

What we know is never anything more than what we know, even if we do not always know it. For a moment the childhod joke about why the chicken crosses the road comes to mind. Suddenly he feels as he did as a child with his first train set. What mattered was to get from one side of the street to the other. All his life he has played by the rules, done what he was supposed to do. Anne may think him distracted, worry about him, but distraction....

the unthought rushing in....

— — —

She sees herself in the desert, nomads in the distance. Wind blows and swirls around her. Sand particles sting her skin. At moments she has to shield her eyes with a hand to see them. Against the immense barren blankness of the desert they are small, insignificant. They must stop at the end of day and camp, but at night in the darkness of her room their night never enters her dream.

Yesterday on the busy street she sees everyday, where she waits for a streetcar after she completes analysis, she had seen them, as if having thought of nomads brought them forth. As if they had escaped the night in which she keeps them from others. The night in which they keep her from others.

—i see nomads in a dream. I follow them at a distance but can't approach them. I don't know why. They are foreign I tell myself. Barbarians.

The weeks she said nothing, words piling up inside her, crowding one another, pushing one another aside. Slippage unintelligible. Borderlines moving constantly. She runs a hand across her forehead.

— — —

It may have been an accident S. placed her hand on his desk but when she abruptly removed it, it was as if she had touched him and was taken aback by what she had done.

It was no accident. She had taken a first step, not knowing what it might be, but could not take the next, knowing what it would mean. His desk was not him but a stand-in for him.

When S. smiled after she had put a hand on his desk he thought of Adriana. A Jew like S. but not at all like her. He heard she'd married, got divorced, left Germany, but there are moments he sees her stand outside his house or wait down the street. She is dusky, slight, with short, curly hair, fierce in her passion for life, mercurial. Anne is not like her. Her family had a place in the world that made a place for him.

As if having put a hand on his desk, S. stood in for Adriana as Adriana does for Anne. As if she

A traceless murmur nowhere but everywhere.

She is at his side. For a moment he wants to put a hand on her shoulder.

— — —

Their faces wrapped in cloths to protect them from the harsh winds of the desert. Only their eyes are visible as she approaches. When she draws close she sees that they follow her without seeming to do so. Their attention that of an animal.

The lead rider waits with what seems an infinite patience for her to come up to them. His eyes dark against a pale headcloth as if they are the eyes of God. Time did not matter to him she thinks. Today is the same as yesterday and tomorrow would be no different than the day before.

All men are men she has seen before, but she is never certain whether the one she sees is the same man or not. It can't be him, but when she sees him she knows who he is. Did she see him first in a book she read as a child? On the lap of father?

Something as complex yet as simple, elementary, as instinct. For a moment she briefly touches her scarf. The day he walked back and forth behind her she saw him at one moment turn at the far corner of the office. His eyes were sunk deep in his head and his forehead lined. He could not look at her but could not look away. Why did Orpheus look back and consign Eurydice to hell?

7

It begins as if it has already begun.
Not when she stood and put a hand on his desk. Before.
When she spoke to him.

Before. Even then.
When she let herself be hypnotized, no longer afraid of
what she would say or what he would think because she had
seen how he struggled with her silence, listened to it, paid
it attention, and understood it turned him away less than
brought him to her.
Before.
The first day she sat down in his office and folded her
hands in her lap.
Before before. When she....
It must have been....
The day a dummy was in father's place in his bed.
It is too soon, too fast.
When she talks into silence.
When she talks into silence she doesn't know where her
words come from.
The last echo of the unspeakable.

— — —

S. leans back against the couch, her hands folded in her
lap. Her eyes are shut and her mouth tightly closed in some
grimace. For a moment she lifts a hand and points it in his
direction before she drops it back to her lap.
Her hands which from the moment she sat down in his
office said what he cannot answer, deny, refuse.

He sees himself stroke her fingers, trace them, follow lines on her palm, touch veins on the top of her hand, bring her hand to his lips, put her fingers in his mouth, suck on them before he lifts her dress, slips her knickers down, raises his hand and brings it down again and again on the reddening skin of her buttocks but it is not his hand which strikes S., but Adriana's which strikes him as he kneels in front of her. Anne lies sleeping alongside him. One of his daughters cries out.

Abruptly he gets up from his desk, looks at S. for a moment before he goes over to the window, looks out. In the street he sees a woman who has stopped a man point down the street, say something. The man gestures with a hand to the left, then to the right. She smiles at him to thank him. She is young, tall, an oval face with delicate scarlet-red lips, cheeks pale red from walking. For a moment the man glances at her as if he is about to say something but only watches her go down the street.

— — —

She was only a child when father left, but once she joined him after so many years away from him, she can never say anything, though there is so much she wants to say. Whenever she tried to speak, the pressure in her head built up, pressed against her so that she could no longer breathe, the pain so intense she had to get up, leave the room, go outside until someone came for her to see if she was all right. Within weeks she had to be hospitalized.

She sees Assia hold her wrist and take her temperature. Still high, she says. I don't know why. It must be something else. She places a hand against her forehead. Assia is a Turk, and Turks don't like to touch Christians, let alone Jews, but she does not seem to mind. She dips a cloth in an aluminum bowl of cold water, squeezes it over the bowl, applies the cloth to her forehead. The fever, if not seizure, woman took with her when she left Paradise. Assia is a woman and women understand one another.

She has to say what she has to say, what she has been unable to say, and when it is said, when she has buried every word that cannot be said. For a moment she sees father look at her before he turns away.

— — —

Down the street a policeman is talking to the barber. A peasant woman carries a baby in her arms. Old Schultz crosses the street painfully. A woman who looks like Anne hurries down the street, her face flushed. He runs a finger down the window, tracing a line through the moisture that has beaded on its glass. For a moment he examines the line his finger has made.

S. wants to help her father as Anne does him, but he will not let her. He has sent her to Berlin for safekeeping. What is best for S. is better for father, even if Berlin is difficult, if not dangerous, for her, the hallucinations taking place on its streets as much hers as Berlin's, as if she belongs to the city, its fever hers, even if she is no more than a shadow darkening one of its walls.

The nomads may stand in for father, but they are not him. The dream tells a story that cannot be told otherwise. She must find a way to read it. She has been away from father so long that the only intimacy with him she has is the patience of her impatience.

— — —

The thought of it is never gone. Whenever it begins it stops. What begins is never a beginning. As humiliating as it is desired. As abject as it is perverse. She needs. God knows she needs but

There it is again. **But** always turns on her, pushes her aside, stops her, says it is for her good.

At the dock, father's eyes clouded over before he hugged her. His lips trembled and he ran a hand across his forehead. He would not look at her. Waves pounded against pier pilings. The crash and ebb of water a force that took her breath away before receding only to rush back with greater force.

Father made everything clear when he would not look at her and passed her along to someone to stand in his place. She was not to be returned packaged to him but stashed away somewhere.

In her dream what at this moment is there in the desert is gone the next. Where the wind buries everything before it. Where here collapses into nowhere and there is always in the distance but never reached.

— — —

Across the street Old Schultz pauses, uncertain whether to go down the block or turn back. He had crossed the street for some reason. He had to get to the other side. He looks back. If he went back, he would pass the man who had crossed to the other side.

He sees himself at home. He kisses Anne on the forehead, asks his daughters how their day had been, reads the paper. It had been he tells Anne. There were. It was not. But nevertheless. Life was. Yes. How could it be otherwise? No.

He has given himself up to work as those who come to him may have done and if it is not work, it is family, church, some passion of one kind or another, but what did not come, did not last and may never have been possible in the first place had broken them. He sees them every day.

Someone traveled inside him, crossing from one side to the other, as if he had brought her with him when he went to the window.

— — —

—When I was a girl, father would ask me to come to the window. He would ask me to tell him what I saw.

She sees his shoulders stiffen. In a moment he leans forward and puts his head against the glass of the window. One hand pushes against the sill.

She runs a hand across her forehead. She glances at the photo of his wife and daughters that he keeps on his desk. What happens as it happened before, but as much as she tries to make it hers, it remains beyond her, out of reach, distant. For a moment she thinks of picking the photo up. Why she does not know.

The weeks she listened to him, followed what he said, she began to feel that they were more alike than she might have guessed, that they shared pasts they could not talk about, wanted what they had not had, thought what could not be said. If she picked the photo up, she would see something she needs to know but had missed. A man. A woman. Children. She thinks of the photo she carries wherever she is. A father. A daughter.

—It was only a game.

Father went to the window to remove himself from himself and see what he could not see from his desk. Windows were doors. Passageways thresholds. He put an arm around her shoulder. She leaned against him. There, she said, pointing. The mourning doves are back. There. Woodchucks, rabbits.

The eagle that describes arcs in the sky above. The chicken on the ground pecking at what comes its way.

— — —

He sees himself at home at breakfast. Anne pours him coffee. His daughters play with their cereal and giggle. Out the window sparrows perch on a wire, as if in a shooting gallery. For a moment — as if it has come a very long way to reach him — he sees his grandfather on the *puszta* plowing a field stop when he sees approach over a rise....

Grandfather never talked about life on the *puszta*. He misses it, mother said. Life on the *puszta* was hard, difficult, but. It's not as if he were free, but on the *puszta* he had something he did not have after he came to the city. Grandmother wanted a more settled life.

—The nomads. Why do you dream of them?

The someone traveling inside him, crossing from one side to the other has been there all along. To reach the other side, as Old Schultz had, he must pass himself going back. His presence at the window is a refusal if not denial of S. as her silence had been of him.

— — —

She does not know what to say. When she first dreamed of nomads, she asked herself why she had. It must mean something. Night after night the dream waited for her until she waited for it.

For her to be with the nomads she thought at first was a sign of her desire to be with father, who had been exiled from Russia and made to live like a nomad. He is not in the desert but he might as well be. The sedentary life he wants long gone.

Father always knew what lay ahead. B follows A. D does not happen unless C is done, but if she is at A, she cannot see B. She cannot make D happen because C tells her only where C is.

Father no longer knows what lay ahead anymore than she does, but persists in believing he does. She may dream of nomads because they, like her, do not know what will come next but, nevertheless, go forward, meet whatever the day brings.

For the first time the woman who is her sits down alongside the woman who is not her and takes her hand. She must leave the couch she says. She cannot be herself on the couch. Father asks us to join him at the window. Windows are to see out. She feels giddy, as she had the day she saw a man watching her while she washed herself. Tightly she grips her hands in her lap.

8

She sees herself lying on a pallet in a tent. The stillness of the night indescribable. Like the turmoil in her head she hears when she is alone and there is no sound but silence which the longer she hears the more deafening it is.

The nomad comes in, leaves food for her. When he enters a second time and lies down beside her, pushes the blanket aside, pulls up her dress, and takes her she knows she has been waiting for him. She put her arms around him, pulled him closer, the insides of her thighs wet, her breath harsh, labored.

This dark night she entered. Its shape, sound, smell known before it was known. She had been no more than a child when she first experienced it, too young to know any words to say what it was, but even now when at unexpected moments it came back, it's coming back as monstrous as it is desired, she cannot say what it is. A present no more than the past brought forward announcing the future.

As if dreams give her license that life did not, even if morning took back what the night had given. The endless litany of why, how could she, it was not possible, she could not, she would never punishing her when she wakes.

Distractedly she looks at H., but sees him as she did at the end of last session, standing at the window, running a finger through moisture that had gathered on the window. When she examined the face of the nomad after they had made love she saw it was the face she sees now. She had forgotten that it was at just that moment she had wakened from the dream until she glanced at H.

She had come to him desolate, abject, desperate, without hope, dragging herself to each session only because she must, holding her pain in her hands like a thing that can be looked at. The missing hand withheld. Never the free hand. Raised.

— — —

S. walks back and forth, gesturing with her hands, talking to herself. At one moment she stops and looks at him, as if she is about to say something. In another she turns away after she had taken a step towards him.

There can be no calm. Not for a Jew on the streets of Berlin whose brown-shirts and homeless, hustlers and hookers go where they go, stop whoever they want. The day he saw S. wait for a tram, the look on her face desolate, abject. As if it would not take her home, but she had to wait for it to carry her where it would.

Calme, du calme. Trains must run on tracks, cars stop when they should, doors shut when they should be shut. Days must begin as they must, end as they should.

There can be no calm. Nothing is what it should be. Not for a man who thought the world was his and whose work is no longer what it was. Whose life is that of a stranger. If there is no law, there can be no justice, but in Berlin today justice is desire, not the law. Life that is no longer life but the only life left. As if everyone is a passenger on a runaway train careening down a track with no emergency brake to pull.

There can be no calm. The word no more than a keepsake that carries in its hand fear in the averted eye, a gut-wrenching tightening in the stomach.

— — —

Come, she had written father, her hand crabbed. Come, she whispered, copying it down. The one word written over and over until the bottom of the page was reached. The only word there was. Her hand spelling it out, writing it down in minute, indecipherable letters.

Father does not come. He does not answer. He does what he does and does does not include her. Who can't but must. Who never would. At one moment she thinks who is her. At another him.

Yet. She can never get beyond yet.

She is his daughter, a Jew like him, as much an exile from Russia as he is. He may acknowledge her, but does not treat her as a father does his child. He may be a Jew but does not know what that means. Russia is for him an idea, not where she was born.

Father she thinks. Family.

Father she thinks. Country.

Father she thinks. History.

She goes to H., takes his hand. He is not father, not family. She no longer has a country. History cannot be re-written. As if his hand in hers gave her assurance that his hand in hers denied him. Her hands know what to do with forks, knives, glasses and plates, buttons, shoes and hats, but at unexpected moments they run away from her, ask her to follow them, catch up, even as she struggles to hold them back, sit on them.

—You are afraid. I am.

Her voice is calm. She cannot be sure she has not imagined what she sees. As if their hands wrapped around one another's were no more than the shadow of hands grasping a future that is itself no more than a shadow of a shadow.

It will begin as it begins. It will end when it ends. Something will happen. Something will not. There is a beginning. The end cannot be known. Tightly she grips his hand. She can do nothing but submit to what she knows she must.

— — —

He runs his fingers over hers, across the back of her hand, turns her hand over, traces lines on her hand as a palm-reader does, but the more he does the more her hand seems to pull him towards her.

For weeks her hands spoke to him and he had not answered. He sat behind her so that she could not see him. He went to the window to keep his distance. His desk sat between them. She had countered by putting her hand on his desk, joining him at the window.

Men must keep women in their place. If a man gives in to a woman he has lost himself. If he lies at her feet, we know what he is. The old, bleary-eyed, rancid men in raincoats he sees shuffling down streets asking for change. Women must submit to men because men have had to submit themselves.

He cradles the back of her head and leans his head on her shoulder. He holds his hand more tightly in hers, as if he did not the world that suddenly had rushed in would no longer be there.

— — —

She pushes her head back against his hand, her hair softly brushing against him, as if her hair is a veil concealing but yet heightening a mystery she does not understand. She touches his cheek.

Storm troopers may be in the street singing the *Horst Wessel Lied*. Thomas, doubting Thomas, may be waiting for her. We must, she hears father say, there is no other choice, but if we don't, then. As if the world goes on as it does, as it must, unaware that she, that he, that they....

Her laugh surprises her. The moment she imagined father say, *but if we don't*, she realizes his *but* always stands in her way. His *but this* a policeman's warning, *but that* a teacher's correction, *but then* the lash of his belt. She laughs again. His *but*. Her buttocks.

Tentatively, shyly, she touches his lip with a finger, tentaively runs the finger across his skin. Almost she thinks but what almost is she does not know only that it be must. He does not flinch or pull back, but once she touches his lips, feels them against her fingers, she cannot help forcing his lips apart, her fingers moving slowly back and forth in his mouth, as if she cannot rush herself, then, suddenly, thrusting them hard, deep into his mouth. His tongue against her fingers is wet, smooth, and in a moment she feels it lick her finger.

She pulls away. The night the dummy in father's bed forced her to kiss him, said he was father, she must love him, and she did, loving father, she did, the taste of goosefeathers suddenly in her mouth.

—It can't be this way. It must be. The weeks here. I saw. You did. It can.

Her words spill over one another. She can't get them out fast enough, as if she did not, they would be lost forever and she would never be able to say them, even if she does not know what the words might be.

— — —

She had come to him with a need she could never satisfy. She had come to him not wanting to come. She had come to him not yet the self that she does not know. The she-not-yet-she had touched his lips and followed where her fingers took her, but it was not until she had done so that she could look at him and it was not until she put her fingers into his mouth that he....

That he.

He had. Had let her. What he.

The look she had given him.

That had. What he would never have.

He goes over to her as if he is sleepwalking, puts a hand on her shoulder as if to calm, comfort her, but in doing so brushes against her breast.

She does not move. Her hands are at rest on her thighs. Her gaze fixed. Burning, burning.

He hears an unearthly music, as if it comes as much from him as it does the room, the street outside, the sky he saw suspended above him when he was a boy. Less sound than a pulse. What he has heard before. What he hears now. What he will always hear. Mourning what has already been lost.

He runs a hand back and forth across her breast and in a moment traces its outline. When he reaches a nipple, it hardens, becomes taut, swollen.

9

She meets who she is to meet. She sits because she is to sit. He is her doctor. He is her lover. She does not look at him. They do not speak.

How it looks is never how it is. Everyone thinks it is the man, but it was not the man. She had pulled him down on the couch, unbuttoned his trousers, took his sex in her hand.

She must face him but cannot manage it. She must decide but any decision has already been made. This woman whose lips went where they did, whose hands touched him as they had. She had clasped her legs around his back, as if she were once again a girl in a cradle father rocked. Had he been the child she rocked? Had she cried out father?

—We don't speak.

As if H. will know she is speaking of the nomad but at this moment she is not sure who we is.

—We have no common language.

The nomad takes her when he takes her. He brings her food when it is time to eat. He puts her behind him on his camel, as if she is no more than some pack. She is not there unless he decides she is. If she....

There was no if. He would use her as he would and discard her when he no longer had any need of her. Once he did the dream that speaks of her night, the night the other side of night, its fear so much a part of her that it has become its intimacy would be gone.

He must say something. Only if he says something, can she, can they.

— — —

What it was was what it was, but it was not what it was. What it was was what the **was** did not say, as if he had not seen her until she pulled him down, unbuttoned his trousers, held his penis in her hand, caressed it, as if it were hers. His erection an insurrection. For a moment he had seen Adriana.

He has done what he would not do. He must account for it but knows the accountability society will exact will never be what it should be. *How can he, that he would, did, does* damning him. Accusations that explain less than judge, which will, for sure, nevertheless, speak, ready to cast the first stone, condemn. That will follow him until

He sees himself in bed lying alongside Anne. He watches himself touch the back of her neck, rub her back, cup her buttocks. She sighs, moves back against him. He does not know whether he asks for forgiveness or if he still loves her. He tucks his head against the back of her neck. Hers to do with him what she will, although who her was.

He cannot be who he is not, but he has. Can. He sees his pen in his hand, the notebook open in front of him. Its page blank. Once the hour is over he makes notes on every patient. He looks at S. Her eyes are closed and hands folded tightly in her lap. Her lips tremble.

—We do talk.

His pen in his hand, the notebook open in front of him. Its page blank.

— — —

The doctor is in. The husband goes home.

The doctor makes love. The husband goes home.

Why did she come? Why does she want this pain? Why does she want him when she knows she cannot have him? Why always wanting why to answer.

She sees herself laid over father's lap, her skirt above her waist, her knickers at her ankles. For a moment she sees him run a hand down his belt, as if he caresses it, before she buries her head in the couch. She waits, but she cannot wait long enough.

Nakedness never as naked.

A wound she must rub.

—You must.

Not knowing what must is, only that it be must.

The nomad rips her dress open, slap her breasts, push her face down onto the floor, take her from behind as a man takes a man. It was not enough. It would never be enough.

— — —

—I must you say. Your father wants life to be must.

She will understand what happened as so many women who come into his office understand it. He said he loved me, but he did not love me. When it came down to it, there was his wife, his children, his job. When it came down to it, there was his reputation, his life. He was sorry he says. So sorry. She will understand he says. She cannot. She wants him. She must have him.

—Life is not always must.

He knows the men they speak of. Bourgeois to the core. Philistines. He has always held himself apart from them, but for him to have done what he has done makes him one of them. It cannot be him, even if it is. The him he can never be. He must keep Anne, her family, his work, give S. up, but if he does not. He sighs a long-drawn out sigh. To argue with himself as those men do not. To. To what? He does not remember what he meant. Whenever he is with them they silence him.

He sees himself in the desert, S. in the distance, as if she has pulled him into her dream. Sand a blind incomprehensible surface. Sky a blunt flatness. Wind harsh, bitter. The expanse endless.

—This has to stop. It's wrong.

As if someone else is speaking. A man not man enough to be a man. Not himself enough to be himself. He touches her shoulder, as if to

She brushes his hand off.

— — —

The weeks she said nothing. Weeks there was no life. Weeks she wanted no more than a hand to console her, a voice to acknowledge her. Wanting only what wanting wants. When mysteriously. As if

Instinct she tells father. Instinct sees in the dark. It hears what can't be heard. There is a moment when. When. You can't ignore it. This has to stop she hears father say, but it is not father who speaks. She puts a hand against her forehead. This has to **STOP, STOP, STOP.** The word chasing after her, pinning her down.

She sees herself sitting apart from the nomads. The desert disappeared into itself. Tomorrow would be the same as today as yesterday had been the same as the day before. Wherever they go they never leave where they are. Every day always a step beyond beyond which

She was no longer alone, even if she would never be one of them. At the same time she felt herself disappearing into herself as much as the desert did every day. The horizon receding farther away the closer you approached it. Suddenly she felt the hand of the nomad on her shoulder. She should not sit by herself.

One can speak, the other cannot.

One could, but did not.

One was the only one but not the only one.

She looks at him, as if he is not the only one she sees, but if she waits long enough it will become clear who he is.

— — —

He goes to her, slowly, step by step, the precipice sheer, headlong, as if no matter how slowly he moves it will not be fast enough.

She bites her lip, presses herself against the back of the couch.

There is nothing he can say. Nothing he can do. Nothing.

He had fumbled with the buttons of her blouse before he freed a breast and took it into his mouth. With a hand at the back of his head, she pulled him to her. Her nipples swollen, wet.

She is no longer who she is. He has ceased to be himself. She fears he will walk away. He fears he will not.

A howl erupts deep inside him, so loud, terrifying that she must hear it, as if it were terror itself that has come into the room.

He kneels and lays his head in her lap.

10

—In the dream it is night. We were returning home with baskets of strawberries. It might have been in Siberia, but I am no longer a child. I'm with a man, but I don't know who he is. A shadowy figure I can't make out.

One day she cannot speak. The next she cannot stop. One day it is a doctor and a patient. The next a man and a woman. One day she sits on the couch. The next his head is in her lap. One day he comes to her room. The next he loosens his belt.

The dream of the nomads gone. It was not until she found herself each night in a vast, desolate desert that she understood that its shifting sands were the only home she had. The place one should escape that had become where she should be. That she pushed away until she could no longer do so. Where she should not go. Where she must. As if the compass pointed north when she was heading south.

—The phone rings. A voice says, he's resting. He's all right. I am distracted, but not only by what the voice said. We had left a basket of strawberries outside. I gesture to the man to go back and get them. It made no sense. At this hour of the night no one would take them.

She does not know who the man is, but when the phone rings, she knew who it was. Father would not call. He writes only when he has to, but wherever she is all she has to do is close her eyes to see him. Whenever she turns around he steps forward. She hears him even when he does not speak.

Something must be wrong with father. In the dream she had looked at the man who had just come back into the house with the strawberries and thought father knows about him .

She sees father at his desk in his study. He writes something down, gets up, paces back and forth, talks to himself, sits down, writes, sits back, examines what he has written, rubs his eyes, leans back, stands, sits, again looks at what he has written.

To be so strong, so great, alone.

Solitude hardened him.

— — —

—Don't worry the voice says. But it wants you to worry. It wants you to answer.

The shadowy figure she can't make out should be him, but she is not sure it is. There is father. She's always seen herself as his. A man she met one afternoon in Berlin.

He sees the doctor passing the lover crossing to the other side, as if for them to acknowledge one another is to threaten both of them. He needs one. He wants the other. But what one does undoes the other.

He looks at S., glances out the window at a bleak gray sky threatening snow. In his notebook he has written S.. A single letter standing by itself. As if it appeared without his having had anything to do with it.

She is the strawberries father has cultivated. She has taken them from him so that she may offer herself to someone else, but does not want him to know.

It is not father. It is him. S. feels she caused him to betray Anne, but cannot say it.

— — —

Father sees them in an office high up in a building in Berlin. Father sees H. approach her. Father sees her trace his lips with a finger. Father sees her look over his shoulder while she lies under him.

It was not father but it was. She'd dreamed of it. She would unloosen his belt, look up at him, show him the love a daughter has for her father, unbutton his fly. She would....

What it is like in the darkness when....

It was not what she thought it would be, but when she'd traced his body with her lips, it was not like anything she. When she took him into her mouth. Tightly she clenches her hands together in her lap.

Her heartbeat is rapid. Suddenly she feels a sharp spasm in her stomach. A fly settles on her hand and she brushes it off. The rising and falling scream of a siren outside.

It was the desert, its shifting sands, harsh sirocco winds. Not her. Not that. But not nothing. The word that must be translated every time it is used. *Rien. Nada. Nichevo. Nient.*

— — —

For weeks he goes to work, goes home, kisses Anne, plays with his daughters, reads, takes notes. They go for walks to the park, zoo, Alexanderplatz. They go to restaurants, opera, theater. One evening Anne says, Something is going on, as if in the weeks everything was the same, nothing was. You talk, she went on, as if it is a recording. You're loving, but you don't love.

He said nothing. There was nothing to say about something that at the time he did not know, but the moment Anne asked about it he began to ask himself if he should. S. has been abandoned by father. He cannot abandon himself. What could they have? He would not be father, even if she would want him to be.

He gets up, sits behind her, as he had in earlier sessions. The man must become the doctor, the woman the patient if things were to be put right. There are moments one must do wrong before one can do right, although how the lover can put on the coat of doctor once he has become lover.

The delicate lines of her neck or long, dark flowing hair

seen as a camera does, its cold gaze running down her neck, touching her hair. Whose surveillance is control. He may ask her questions, comment as those who speak from behind a curtain do. Whose voice is power.

She knows he is there, but can do nothing about it. She can only wait for him to do or say something without being aware of what he is doing while her thoughts chase after themselves but never catch up. He needs to. For a moment he rubs his forehead.

Her long black hair brushes the back of the couch. Her shoulders are rigid. For a moment she touches a hoop earring. This woman who had been all woman, done what she will, thrown restraint to the winds no more than a grave one visits on All Soul's Day.

He goes over to her, puts his hands on her shoulders, as if he watches someone else. The fantasy he walks through alone.

The man throws his life away for love. The woman gives herself up to give herself up. The man who loves children, tends flowers, pets cats one day stabs his wife. The woman poisons the man she loves because he no longer loves her.

— — —

His fingers touch the hard bone of the clavicle, the thick muscles of her shoulder and neck, brush against her pronounced, blunt forehead, trace sharp, Slavic cheeks.

Their hands.

Always their hands.

That reassure, encourage, desire, console.

That punish, insist, demand.

That say what she needs, wants.

She cannot be herself as long as their hands go where they go, do what they do. Suddenly she pulls away from him.

—Don't.

Abruptly she gets up, goes to the window. The skin of her neck stings. Her cheeks are hot. For a moment she puts a hand on the sill to steady herself.

On the street several middle-aged women go by with grocery bags in hand. At the corner a legless man holds out a cup. A woman wheels a baby carriage down the street. A fashionably dressed young woman stops for a moment and looks up at something in the building across the street. Something that has caught her attention. A face in the window. A bird on a ledge.

It would not be enough.

It would never be enough.

— — —

He stands behind the couch, his hands resting on it. She leans forward, one hand on the window sill. As if they must wait for someone to clap his hands, a voice say something, whoever or whatever it is that directs our lives point the way before he can move from the couch, she from the window.

What we want should be what we can have, but it cannot be. Everyday they come to his office because it cannot be. Why they ask. For a moment he sees his grandfather sitting by the fire. He never said anything. There was no life for him in Berlin. He misses the *puszta*, but loved grandma. She wanted to be in Berlin.

The voice he should hear, the one he always hears, the one he needs to hear does not speak, but for a moment he turns as if he has heard something. He sees grandfather sitting silently by the fire.

When he turns back he sees his hand on S.'s shoulder. For a moment her shoulders tense before she leans back against him. He has not crossed the room to the window but thinks he has. He has never felt more alone than he does now.

— — —

A young man in overalls and leather jacket approaches the woman who had stopped when she saw something, asks her something, she answers, gestures to the left, then to the right, he thanks her, takes a step away from her, stops, comes back, says something, she nods.

A half-dozen brown shirts come down the street One smashes a store window with a lead pipe. Another paints **No Jews!** on a wall. A boy runs up to be with them. The woman with the baby carriage bends over her child. An old man watches them. His glance impassive.

Yesterday she had seen a worker beaten by brownshirts. She had gone up to him afterward, asked if he were all right, could she do something. He said nothing, only wiped his bloody lips, spat out some teeth, looked at her indifferently before he got up. She was a foreigner. Perhaps he thought a Jew. She remembers thin lips, dark stubble on his cheeks, cold eyes.

Everyday she tells herself father must see this, he must know what it is like, but she does not write and even if she did, he would not answer. There are so many things he has to do, so many people to see, so much to write.

The words in her mouth never say what she wants them to say as if they wait for her to say them so that they can betray her, but even if she says nothing, the murmur of her hands, the cry of her heart, the silence of her gaze haunt her.

— — —

Grandfather was never at home in Berlin, but he loved grandmother and what she wanted was enough. He loves Anne and his daughters but sees them as if he is sitting at the back of a theatre watching a home movie of someone else's life. Anne sits on the couch knitting. His daughters play with dolls. He looks for himself on the screen but the homburg he hangs on the hat rack in the vestibule when he comes home is not there. Suddenly he feels her hand touch his cheek.

Every day S. sees brown shirts come down the street. One day she knows they will see her. She thinks that he. If he would. She can

He can do nothing. A threshold becomes a boundary. Borders keep us in check. The unspeakable everyday a margin no language can describe. He clasps her hand against his cheek.

Delicate hairs of her hand, pronounced veins, a minute, ridged scar brush up against him. Her breath a whisper. The most foreign land. Where we go when we can go nowhere else.

11

—I saw a man beaten.

She did not know life. Would never know it. The guilty dream she has about those who have less than her, who suffer as she has not, even if what she has is little, every day less, not much, hardly anything. She belongs with them but has never felt at ease with anyone but father. She lacks something. Does not have whatever it is. As much as father taught her.

She is not one of those women who drop coins in beggars' cups or bring food to the homeless and tell their friends over tea about it afterward. So sad they sigh. Them. They always call them them. They are never them.

—I can't get him out of my head.

She is who she is. She has walked in its tracks since she can first remember. For a moment she sees Thomas, doubting Thomas, waiting for her on the street. She has not seen him in weeks. It was not that she no longer looked for him. She never did. He found her. Knew where she would be. Whenever she saw him she knew that they were them.

— — —

That rabble Anne says. He never knows whether she means communists or Nazis. They may be Germans she says but they are not German. They don't know their place.

He did not answer Anne. He shrugged his shoulders, smiled weakly. Vertical invaders Ortega y Gasset calls them. Those who step on the stage of history and don't belong there. He did not want to get into it with her. Anything he might say would be misunderstood.

—That man.

If her family gave him a respectability he would not

otherwise have, he made it possible for her to live as she should. Her family was not what it once was. The bourgeois she says as if it were a curse. At moments he did not know whether she loved him, but knows love matters less to her than her place in life.

—He may be anywhere. The Nazis say he is everywhere.

S. had brought the man into the room but did so not to put him but herself at his feet. When she saw him beaten she saw herself. She is a Jew. Nazis know what Jews are.

—He is nowhere but every day he is singled out, beaten, taken away.

They know she seduced him in an effort to save herself. They know she seduced him because that is how Jews are. She cannot ask him to choose, but if he loves her

—We cannot speak of him because to do so is to speak of the unspeakable. We cannot speak of him because to do so is to say what no one wants to hear. We cannot speak of him because to do so is to become him.

He cannot be who she wants him to be. The him the Nazis will hunt if they know about them.

— — —

—I can't forget him.

As if she is, somehow, complicit. She'd seen him beaten and could not help. She is complicit. For weeks she's wanted to tell someone about H. The prostitute in her building she nods to when they see one another at the mail box. The waitress at the café where she stops for coffee who worries about her because she is never with a man. If he would only say, there is a woman, S.

Every day on the streets of Berlin she sees the choices women have made, the decisions they have reached, the lives they live. She sees it in what they wear, how they walk. She hears it in what they say. She can't get the sounds of their voices out of her head. To live is to be complicit.

She is not his kind. She did not understand, could not know what it was like for that man to live as he does.

She is not any kind. Those who have know she is a have not. Those who have nothing know she has what they do not. Her place — whatever place she has — has no relation to what is inside her.

Anyone. Anyone of them. She puts her head in her hands. She wants to be one of them. She is the one to be put down. The one who never stands up. Who offers herself. She knows. God she knows.

The whip comes down. Lash after lash. Again, again. Its sting that she needs.

— — —

Something is going on, Anne says. If it does not stop. I don't care who she is. One of your patients. The maid. It's not them I worry about. They're nothing but a distraction. It's you. When you look at me you no longer see me. I won't have a man do that to me.

She talks about another woman to talk about herself. At a dinner last week he saw her lips tighten when a man she had known a long time ignored her for the young wife of a colleague. When an elderly uncle patted her on the shoulder she winced. She is not old but had not thought about herself before as not young.

He did not answer Anne. He does not answer S. He cannot be for one what he is not for the other. He can leave S. That he can gives him the assurance he needs for him to stay. He cannot leave Anne. That he cannot makes him want to flee.

Mornings he sees himself in the mirror while he shaves.

For a moment he pauses, holding the razor in his hand. The face in the mirror does not turn away as his does every day.

It cannot last. Because. He rubs his eyes. Because always the defense of the one who cannot, will not, won't.

He sees S. standing in the middle of the room, uncertain whether to go or to stay. He goes to her, cradles her head in his hands, kisses her. Her lips are soft, yielding, but there is no desire in his kiss, only the need of one who has never felt more alone.

— — —

His kiss at first passive, as if he only rested his lips against hers, soon becomes urgent if not frantic, forcing her lips open, thrusting his tongue deep into her mouth before he pulls away.

She won't make it. She'll never make it. Day after day is the same. Every day begins as yesterday had. Every day stops less than pauses. They may call it life but she knows what it is. She buries her head against his chest.

Night after night darkness gives back what the day took. She holds desire in hand. She touches her lips to feel where his have been. As much as he is to her during the day. She cannot stop. He can never be to her what he is under the covers. She cannot sleep. Before night ends. Day begin.

The beat of his heart is even, steady, as her is not. She pulls him closer, runs her hands down his back. She is not a woman who uses her body to trap men. She knows what happens to those women. Their bodies may get them what they want but cannot keep it. They are used. They can be used again. The delivery boy. The postman. A clerk. She rubs her nose against his chest like a small animal seeking warmth.

She may not have been the first patient he's slept with.

They come to him troubled, uncertain, desolate. They have failed. Not got what life promised. Only he can help. They can no longer live. They've tried everything. They are young, attractive.

The more her thoughts backtrack endlessly on themselves the more an abyss opens. She does not want to know. She won't be able to take what she might find out. She won't. She may go up to the edge but she won't look over.

She hears a murmuring. The low, repetitive, chant she heard for weeks in her dream. In the desert, at the end of day, near dusk, nomads kneeling at prayer, facing east, raising their hands up, bending their heads to the ground.

She stood aside. She could not kneel. She could not pray.

— — —

He does not want to say anything, does not want to think, wants no more than to remove himself from himself, but the more he does the more images rush in to fill the place he has left. A dizzying, kaleidoscopic spectacle.

He sees grandfather sitting at the side of the stove, his face ashen, gray, eyes sunken in his head, the skin of his forehead stretched thin. Say something to him, mother says. Tell him about school, what you study, when you went to Wansee last summer, the fish you caught.

He remembers seeing photos of grandfather as a young man. In one photo, he stands, facing the camera, a blunt chin, a dark, thick handlebar moustache, piercing eyes. On the *puszta*. At the edge of the world.

In another photo taken in some studio, he stands alongside grandmother, the two of them stiff, uncomfortable. He wears a white jersey, vest, hat. She a kerchief, crocheted blouse, full skirt. They stare guardedly at the camera as if it examines them as a policeman does.

He sees Anne when he first met her. She had long, straw-blonde hair wrapped in a bun, emerald green eyes, a shy smile. Girlish. Not yet the woman who would see the world, go to Venice, Athens, Cairo, talk of the Lido, the Parthenon, Giza. He had gone no farther than Vienna and at moments did not know what she made of him.

You are, she said when they met. He did not know how to answer. He did not need to know who she was. Everyone knew her family.

He sees Anne lying under him the day he first took her in the woods outside Berlin. Her eyes are shut, cheeks red, perspiration beads her forehead. A smile of satisfaction on her face. He touches her breast, cups it, as if he must hold it in his hand to make it real.

Adriana comes up. I see how you look at me, she says. She runs a finger down his cheek. You want me. She laughs. You are afraid.

Adriana comes back. So? she asks. You would not follow me, but you do her. For a moment she holds his chin in her hand. You will follow her, even after she is gone. She turns away from him.

— — —

The weeks she'd followed nomads in the desert she'd come to understand the dream to be her life. Over the next dune, she thought, always thought, there would be life, but once she reached the top of the next rise there was nothing — never anything — on the other side.

Once she'd joined the nomads her world was no longer what it was. It must have been the next session she put a hand on H.s desk to steady herself, inadvertently she thought, but she knew, nevertheless, that things were not the same. Not since childhood. Before father left.

She pulls him closer. As if she is once again standing alongside father at the window. She does not know how it happened. It was not her. It sought her out and she'd not turned away from it, as father had when she saw him after so many years without him. She rubs her nose against his chest.

—It can't go on like this. You know that.

She runs fingers through his hair, touches his neck, pulls him closer.

—You'll lose your life. I can't ask you to do that.

On the ledge outside the window a pigeon perches. A hard rain beats against the window. She can't remember the last time she saw the sun. Time passes. Life goes on. But it doesn't. It stops when you want it to continue. It rushes forward when you want to stop it.

—What do you want? Tell me.

The first day in the office she stood at the door, motionless.

He pointed to the couch. That's where she would sit. She sat.

The second day he asked why she did not speak.

She said nothing.

The third he sat behind her so she would not see him.

She could not get him out of her thoughts.

The fourth she knew it would not help.

Father sent her to Berlin so that she would not get in his way. She wanted to run.

The fifth he listened.

To listen is to hear without hearing. He spoke.

The sixth he waited.

To wait is to stop without stopping. She had not run.

12

They come. In the morning they come. Only in darkness can their mission be done. While everyone sleeps no one will see them and if they do they will think it a dream.

They will not find father. The man they will find is no more than a dummy he has put in his bed for everyone to think he is here. She'd come crying into the kitchen when she saw it was not father in bed. He had to go, mother said. It was time. He was no longer safe. He has to. Go outside. Play. You should not be here.

She sees soldiers. She sees soldiers enter their home. It is quiet. Silence a stain. She sees soldiers. Silence suddenly broken by the harsh cries of a jay. The day waits. No more than a pause.

Gunfire. A rattattat burst stitching its way across the morning. It cannot have been more than a few seconds. What had not been there before would now be brought back by a shout in the street, a cry in the night, a door closing. She sees soldiers. She will always see soldiers. She who had been left waiting.

It is father on the stretcher. His eyes stare vacantly. His chest hemorraghes blood. One of the soldiers smiles, sheepish, nevous. Another turns away. A third wipes his brow. They have done what they were to do.

Children and one or two women have gathered outside the building. High in the sky, a hawk floats. She covers her mouth. They may not know who she is. She looks away. At the edge of a field, a rabbit stops. A sparrow perches on the branch of a tree. She sees an officer glance at her. They do.

She runs. She does not know how long she'd run, where she'd gone and what she saw, but she cannot have run far enough to escape the sight of father on the stretcher, his gaze empty, chest bloody, mouth hanging open, as if he is surprised.

When she comes back it is midday. No one says anything. Children — some of them her friends — turn away. The soldiers have gone. She goes into the building. Mother is in the bedroom. She rushes over to her and throws herself on her lap. Mother's hand strokes her head. Back and forth her hand moves. Back and forth.

Yesterday had been a day like any other. Today would always be the day she saw father dead. Every day now she will see a headline in a paper, hear a voice on the street, feel a hand on her shoulder with the news. The man she always hears who one day she will hear no more.

Father turns towards her from the window in his office. He beckons for her to join him.

— — —

Her eyes are large in her head, shining, wet. She looks at him but does not see him. Her blank gaze a drawn shade. For a moment she puts a hand over her mouth. A muffled cry escapes her. She clasps her hands in her lap.

He'd been to her room. Sat on a bench in a park with her. One day they had gone to a lake. He would not meet her at a café. I know you can't be seen with me, she says. I understand. But. We've crossed a line and once we did it can't be hidden.

She was no longer at ease in the office. In the office, she says. In the office, I am a patient. You are a doctor. If it had not been for you. But now. It's not as if I no longer need analysis. It's just. To be in the office is to step back.

Today she has come to the office to be a patient. It was something other than feeling threatened to be seen with him, fearing for him rather than herself or what her neighbors thought when he entered and left her room.

He sees her wait for a tram. Her eyes lidded, dark shadows under them, face drawn, strained, shoulders bent. She knows she has to take the tram, but fears where it will take her. She walks back and forth, back and forth, looks down the street, impatient for the tram to arrive and take her where it will as quickly as possible. She is tired. There is nothing she can do. She wants to get it over.

— — —

She wants him to say something. It does not matter what. Just to hear his voice. The one she hears when she buries her head in the pillow at night. The one that talks to her over *chai* in the morning. He should be here when she needs him, and if he is not, he should let her go. At least the anguish of loss is clear.

She sees father sit up on the stretcher and look around. For the first time he sees the world the way it is. For the first time understands how it sees him. When he sees her, he falls back. For the first time he judges himself.

On the quai while she waited for the ferry to the mainland and the train that would take her to Berlin, he put his arms around her in an awkward embrace. She was his daughter but he held her away from him, looked at her she thought as if to remember who she was.

He said nothing. There was no right word. There could be none.

Waves washed gently against pier pilings. Gulls wheeled and turned in the sky, dove down to the water. The sun disappeared behind a cloud. Father growing smaller and smaller on the quay.

— — —

He pulls her towards him, takes her hands.

I hear what they say, Anne says. How can you? A Jew. I don't want to believe it, but if it's true, you're done, finished. I can't believe you would do this. They told me you were like Franz. Living in Paris with a whore. Abuptly she laughed. I wouldn't believe them. That was not you I said. Franz may be family but he was not blood. What did I know?

One night she comes to him drunk, in tears. What does she do? she asks. Suck your cock? Wants to be fucked in the ass? She slaps him across the face. I bet you whip her. I know you would whip me. You've always felt my family looks down on you. To get back at me is to get back at them. Hysterically she laughs. You haven't the balls.

Flesh speaks. Flesh seeks. He buries himself between S.'s legs as he never did with Anne. If she were to ask him to lick her boots, he would not hesitate, even if he holds back, keeps in what needs to be kept in until he no longer can.

He cannot be without her but cannot be with her, even if at moments he thinks it is Anne he cannot be without.

— — —

Tightly she grips his hands.

She must want father dead. For weeks she stared into its face. As long as father is alive she will never be free, but she cannot let him go. Without him there is no life.

It had been difficult to be with father. She had not seen him since she was a child. Whatever she did undid itself. She was nervous, not well. He had no patience. The doctor will help, he said. I can do nothing. It will only be for a short time.

If she is in Berlin, he does not have to see her. If she writes, he does not have to answer. What was best for her was better for him.

For weeks she did nothing. One day she saw a man see

her naked in the bathroom. One day she began dreaming of nomads in the desert. One day she put a hand on his desk. She who would not say anything had spoken.

Then.

At first she did not recognize it. Then she knew that then. She could not miss it.

That he. That she. That they.

Until.

She goes over it in her mind. She does not know how to explain it. The more they came together, the more that whatever they had was, more than she ever could have guessed, the more the world they kept out came back.

It was not that when anyone saw them together she thought they know what's going on. A bourgeois German with a foreign Jewess. She did not care about that. What anyone thought was not their business.

It was what she could not do but had, as if she could not do it fast enough that spoke for the world. It sat with her.

Thou shalt. The word of the Father.

The last time she said father she could not get the word out. *Fa* she said. *Fath. Ffa.*

— — —

He sees grandfather sitting by the fire. Anne walks back and forth, back and forth. S.'s father turns from the window. He hears a shout in the street.

Family. They never let you go.

Berlin. It knocks on your door.

Germany. You are one of us.

A father with children. A psychoanalyst in the city. A citizen. He is one of them, but if he is not, Anne will leave him, someone who has seen them go to the police. The not-one-of-them pays always pays.

He can go back to Anne. She would make life difficult for him, but would not leave. S. had nowhere to go. Father does not want her. If he is no longer with her. A Jew in Berlin without family or friend.

They'd rushed down a path without looking around, without thinking where it led, as surely they must have known where it would. If there were a way to forget what had been written for all to see, dismiss it, say he should have known better....

They come to him everyday. It can be done, can't it? There must be something. They will risk what they would not before. The situation in Germany will change. They will get better.

There was nothing. He must live with it, nevertheless, however he can.

He lifts her hands to his mouth, kisses them.

13

She loves a man. She does not know who he is or where she met him. At moments he is a stranger. He is there when she least expects him, but when she wants him to be there, she cannot find him. She must run her hand across his forehead, trace his cheeks, touch his lips to convince herself he is real. At first she mistook him for father.

She remembers she'd been with father. She'd not seen him for more than twenty years. Things had not gone well. Her chest hurt. She had headaches. At times she cried. She should have been Nina. If she were Nina

Everyone said rest. You're not well. Father has work to do. You should not bother him. Go down to the shore. The sea is blue. A blue we have not seen before.

At the shore waves washed gently against rocks. Gulls edged near, waiting for crumbs. The sky was gray, always gray. One day a man appeared over the rise and beckoned to her. She went with him. She does not remember what happened. At dusk they found her.

When she got up this morning, she asked herself where she was. She must know but did not. She dressed, went out to look for a café to have *chai*. She might see something that would tell her where she is. She might see someone she knew, a shop she recognized, some landmark.

A grocer asks how she is. At the post office they say, no. No letter today. The sign over a café said *Berliner*. Inside a waiter nods. The man she loves must be one of the men she sees there.

— — —

When she saw him she was startled, as if she did not know someone would be here. She turns, takes a step towards the door, but stops, turns back to make sure she does not know him.

—You've been here before.

The weeks S. was no more than a patient. Weeks she did not speak her hands wrestled with themselves in her lap, her legs crossed and uncrossed themselves.

—You came to the door. You opened it.

The day she put a hand on his desk he knew what it was.

The day she turned away from the window to see if he would join her he knew he must answer.

—There must have been a reason.

Nights he lies alongside Anne, S. slips into bed with them. He remembers her hands coiling around themselves like snakes in a pit, one leg sliding across the other. How could she have done this? It was not like her. For so long she held back, always held back, until she could no longer hold in what had been building up inside her and rushed in, as if she must act before it was lost.

She knows he will not take the next step. She had come to him no longer able to live. How is it possible to live without a father's love? She knew he would be like father, but had come to him nevertheless.

—Sit down. Rest. It will come back to you.

She who could not speak. Who had been abandoned. He who was silenced. A stranger to himself. She put a hand on his desk. He saw the hand as if it were a footprint in the sand. What had begun without a beginning could not be put aside.

He is not lying alongside Anne. It is no longer night. S. is beside him. Her head against his chest, her hands at his hips, her thighs touching his.

— — —

The man she loves is not this man. At moments she thinks it is not any man. She made him up. If he were real, she'd run away. If he were a man, he would not love her. It is better, far better, that a man she cannot know loves her. He will not leave, but if he does, what will — can — she have lost? A man not there in the first place.

Suddenly she is no longer in a room three stories up in a building in a Berlin but somewhere in the middle of the desert that she must have traveled a long time to reach. She sees father. He must be waiting for her. She approaches him.

Everything happens so fast now she cannot make out what is going on. She sees a bottle of vodka in her hand. She sees the man she saw in the office. He nods. She douses father with the alcohol. She turns back to the man, unsure what to do next. He hands her a match.

Father smolders, burns, bursts into flames. No more than a car wreck left at the side of a busy highway. A warning. Flames spread quickly across the sand, lick against her as the kisses of a lover do, burning, insistent. The man who would be a torch to lead people into a new world.

She rushes up to him. She must smother the fire, put it out, but when she crushes father to her breast she knows it is not the fire she wants to put out. The torch she can no longer hold, but cannot escape must burn down.

Father should have.

He did not.

He left.

He did not look back.

He.

HeeHeeHee.

She laughs, hysterical. She can't help herself, abject. She holds her hands up, desolate.

—I don't know who you are.

113

It is father she speaks of. It is the man she loves. Not the man who hears what she has just said, but if she did not want him to hear it, why did she say it?

He must know, but why should he know, even if what he must know she does not? As if she had stopped him like a drunk on the street does. You've got to listen, he says. You must know. Someone must.

Ashes. There are ashes.

— — —

She speaks as if it his voice she speaks through. As if he does not know who he is, has never known, but can only discover himself through her voice that sings as a bird in a cage does.

He must go, somehow, to the place she is, but does not know whether he must — or can — bring her back or remain with her in the place she has but does not have.

Yesterday he got on a tram and took the only seat left, next to a man in overalls and pea-coat, wearing a worker's cap. His shoes were hob-nailed boots. The man edged over to give him room.

Anne had asked him to stop at the grocer's. He had to pick up medication at the chemist's for one daughter. For a moment he thought of S. He must do something. If at one moment it is clear what he must do, at the next he knows it is not possible.

He does not know why he felt the man examined him. He knows who he is. He knows he is kept in his place by those like him. If it it had not been for him they say. If it were not for them. As if they must rub the scar.

At the next stop, the man bumped him when he got up, excused himself, stepped around him and went down to the exit. He nodded to an old, Slavic-looking woman holding a cloth bag who was standing in the aisle. *Stoda-babas* they call them. The woman looked at him.

The man's shoulder brushing against him foreshadowing the time to come.

He sits by S., takes her hand. She leans against his shoulder, puts a hand on top of theirs.

— — —

She is S. She is in Berlin. She has gone for a walk. She stopped at this building. She's seen it before. She entered, walked up not one, but two, three flights of stairs. She did not hesitate. She stopped at this door, not any other, opened it, entered.

She must know the office That must be why she stopped at this building, walked up the stairs, came to this door. She must know the man. He was not surprised when he saw her.

There must be a reason she is here. He must belong here since he is here. Whoever he is and whatever he does leads him to this office. She does not remember where she was yesterday nor what she did but whatever it was had led her here too. He knows what she must know as she does not. She sees herself as she saw herself in the dream in the desert drawing close to nomads.

—Are you the man I love?

She must believe what she believes, even if at moments a gulf widens. She is in Berlin. She loves a man, but not to know who he is, let alone herself is a dizzying vertigo. The familiar no longer itself can never be familiar again.

She rubs her nose against his shoulder, tightens his hand on hers. Waiting for what happened to happen.

SOME DO,
SOME DO NOT

It's music you want to capture the evening, but most of the time it doesn't work. At some point you realize you have not listened. You make more of an effort to follow and then it stops, the evening ends, and you have missed what drew you there in the first place, what, you are not exactly certain. It might have been there, but it went by you.

Sharp, smooth cheeks with the prominent cheekbones of the Slav or Asian, nose tilted up at the end, thin, delicate lips, a nondescript chin that shaped a face less than disappeared into the neck. Her hair is sandy-brown, curly, cut short. Her eyes pale green, transparent, flecked with gray. She is absorbed by the music but seems distracted. She bites her lip. For a moment she shuts her eyes. Eyelids dark lavender, vulnerable.

You must enter the music before it can enter you. Before it can send you down a path, cut a trail for you. The bass carrying the beat. The tenor sax chasing itself. Drums crashing. Days and weeks and years of work and evenings out to restore the balance. Written on your skin, shaping memory and dream. It does not happen every night and when it does you know why you search it out. The evening she leaned across the table and brushed her lips against yours, caressed your hand, smiled with desire, happy. *Waltz for Debby* brushed up against you, Motian's bass riff solo.

Not the place to draw a jazz crowd. Montreal is a tough city for any business to make it, and the hotel has to have a restaurant, a bar, music to keep up. Live jazz is more upscale than muzak, but the trio is young, college students earning money on the side. People drift down from their rooms in the hotel for a drink or meal, because they are reluctant to go outside in a strange city at night. Or they've been on the road a long time and are beat, but they're in a city and should do something. They can't tell friends they were in Montreal and did not do anything. Others drop in, not sure why, other than it's Friday night and they need to be out. Jazz? Why not? Friends of the band come in. Some of them would just as soon be elsewhere. But friends are friends. One night something may happen. You never know what. Even an evening like this one. So they go out, come in. Then are there those who know nothing ever happens, but they have to be out anyway, alone in a crowd.

His head shaved, a hoop earring, dark, thick moustache. Shining chestnut-brown eyes under bushy brows, strong chin jutting forward. His glasses do not have frames, which gives his face the look of a sepia photograph at the turn of the century. He appears tired, his face drawn. For a moment he takes his glasses off, rubs his eyes, runs a finger across his moustache. He looks at the band, around the restaurant, at the woman at the table next to him, drains his beer.

The place is important. One has to see and be seen. One does not care to be seen, does not want to be recognized. The place is not important. It can be anywhere. It does not matter. The place is important. It has to be away from home, out. Wherever it might be is always the place one is in and tonight it is better than home, an apartment, a hotel room, even if it is not a bar to tell anyone about, make a story of, just somewhere to stop one night of your life.

Have we not seen her before? In another city, another country, another life? The drummer finishes his riff with an exaggerated crescendo, and she smiles, teeth brilliant, white, perfect. For a moment she looks down at the table and runs a finger around the lip of her wine glass. The waitress comes by and asks if she wants another glass of wine and she shakes her head no. There is the next set, the evening still young, yet to wend its way to the end of night.

You have to be polite her mother always said. You must be pleasant, courteous, agreeable. Remember to smile. Everyone likes the one who smiles. You do not want to make anyone angry, but you must be clear, firm if you need to be. Just because someone asks you something you do not have to say yes. "*Merci,*" she says. "*Mais no. Peut-etre plus tard.*" She gives the waitress a smile. Her mother taught her well. She has learned to say no when she means no, but sometimes no one hears or pays attention, particularly men. When men don't want to hear no, they don't hear it. She may not have enough money. She may not want to drink more. She may want to be alone, not bothered. It is no one's business. The waitress has a job, and she must reply when the waitress asks if the food is all right, does she want another drink, is there anything she needs. The walls of the woman's home, the face of her husband or lover may have long ceased to say anything. Tonight she may need to hear the sound of her own voice.

She is attractive. Lean, muscular legs in a mini-skirt and boots. The sharp, angular cheeks of the Slav. Pale green eyes flecked with hazel-gray. In her forties. The jazz trio is young and she might be a mother of one of them. She must struggle to make ends meet. Her boots are imitation leather, cracked in places, her panty-hose badly stretched, her beige mini-skirt and pale blue sweater embroidered with flowers at the breast from some cheap outlet mall. You like the music? he might begin. You come here often? You. It has to begin with you. A man at a table alone. A woman at a table alone. The story s obvious, clear, in one telling of it. A man at a table alone. A woman at a table alone. A man and a woman sitting together, talking, deciding. A man and a woman leaving together. As much as stories are always what people believe them to be, they are never what they seem. You go out to get away from home. You go out to be alone in a crowd. You go out in search of talk. You go out not to be bothered by the man sitting alone at the table next to yours, not to be bothered by the woman sitting alone at the table next to yours. The talk is rarely talk. Just something to say you are there. Some say nothing and look down at their drinks. Some cannot shut up because they don't know what to say.

She put her suitcase down in the train station in Leningrad and looked for a place to sit. In front of her a Soviet soldier sat on his trunk, legs crossed, and looked at something behind her. A cape hung from one shoulder and he wore freshly-polished knee-high boots. His gloved hands are folded on one thigh. A medal is pinned to his jersey. His short, blond hair is tousled. He is young, but knows what his life will be. Everyone sees it in the way he sits, looks around, stretches. What her life might be she cannot guess. She just knows it cannot be in Russia. Behind the soldier, a young man in a pea-coat with long, unkempt hair looked dully at the soldier. In a moment he turned away. His hair is long, too long for Russia, and life not easy. There are hundreds of passengers sitting or standing waiting for trains, but no place where she might rest. She touches the suitcase with her foot to make certain it is still there. She has come this far. She must take the next step. Everyone has a reason to be here, a ticket to take them away, but they sit waiting, as they have done most of their lives. For a moment she looked at one face, then another on a bench, followed faces down a row, down the next one. No one talked. Some sat with eyes shut. Others fingered objects in their hands. She picked her suitcase up and walked across the tile floor to the trains. Like them she had a ticket in her purse, a place to go. Helsinki. West across the Neva, circling the Gulf of Finland. Reykjavik. Where the plane from Helsinki touched down. Montreal. An uncle.

The music can speak to you, lift you up, say this is life, this is how it can be, time no longer time, only the moment of this moment, your mind free, roaming at will, soaring above fields and streams, towns and roads, sound brushing up against you, ruffling your hair, quickening your pulse. Here the music says. You must be here. Inside me you will be inside yourself.

He frowns and his forehead creases. He runs a hand across his bald head, glances at the woman at the table next to his, looks away. At the bar the chef in a tight white smock talks to the manager and bartender, a heavy-set woman in her late forties. The music does nothing for him. Like a conversation that causes the mind to drift, his glance to stray. It's not even noise. He notices it as he might an air conditioner or fan. Every now and then he becomes aware of the sax or bass, makes another effort to listen, but it makes no impression. At least noise makes itself heard. Some days after a deadening day in the office he would settle for noise. He rubs his eyes and grimaces. His cheeks still bear the marks of teenage acne. Sometimes noise is the only message that gets through. During the Algerian revolution, the French blocked the FLN radio with static, but Algerians listened anyway. As long as there was static the resistance was alive.

Antoine said he loved me, said he wanted to spend the rest of his life with me. Do you know how I feel, he said, when I feel your lips against mine, your breast in my mouth, my cock inside you? I had been in Montreal less than two months. I was 18. I did not know what to wear, how to talk, but he taught me what I needed to know. I wrote my aunt in Leningrad. It's not like anything I thought it would be. I knew I had to leave. Sergei's family wanted nothing to do with me. They kept at it, rubbed my nose in it. Look, Sergei. She's not educated. She's not from a good family. Those kind of women trap you. You work hard and she just wants to be set up nicely. It was not easy. Ludmila told me about a loophole in regulations, but I had to pay officials before they would do anything. Don't ask me how. I thought Canada was like Europe, but it's not. It's so unlike anything I thought it might be. The books call it the new world, *tetya*, and it is. You would not believe what I see walking down the main street, St. Catherine. At each block there's a story. At each corner a life.

One day in Palmer Park when he was 15, he looked around from the bench he sat on. Ducks glided across a pond. A father played catch with his son. The ball sailed back and forth between them under a clear azure sky. Boys cycled down a path. The breath of a breeze. He heard racquet against ball in tennis courts nearby. Detroit was the world. Today he cannot think of a place he can live. Work keeps him anchored. Sometimes it pushes him on, passes him along. Some days he sits at his desk and asks himself how much longer he can sit there. Every day the bucket goes to the well, Bob Marley sings, and one day the bottom will drop out. He waits for the moment. Marriage did not, after ten years, keep him. He has had to put in frequent-flyer miles from family. For more than a decade now he has been in one place. He asks the clerk at the post office about her grandchildren. He asks the girl at the quick-stop about her husband in Iraq. He has grown tired of packing, pulling up stakes, moving. Home may be Detroit, where he was born. Home may be the center of one's universe, but he has never found it. He has memories, and if that be home, he does not talk about them.

He traces a straight line on the table cloth. For a moment he examines the linen of the cloth, spotted with rust stains cleaners could not eliminate. In several places the linen has been repaired. He draws another line, a third. His glance intent on his finger. The veins on the back of his hand are thick, pronounced, and the skin dark, wrinkled. He folds his hands together on the table and stretches back in his chair. The beat of the bass staccato. His gaze intent on the trio while he waits for the moment he will turn to her and speak. The

Robert Buckeye

walls of his hotel room stared back at him. The newspaper
did not interest him. He needed to be in a crowd, and if not
find someone to talk to, at least not be alone.

Every story unfolds. Whenever Antoine wanted me, I put
everything aside. When he smiled, I was happy, so happy.
When he laughed, I laughed. That was 27 years ago. He's
remarried, has three children, still calls. There will never be
anyone like you, he says. Later in the evening she will tell the
story to the man at the table next to hers. She needs to tell it
and rehearses it in her mind. She looks at him. He seems to
like the music. He has a strong jaw, looks fierce, but his eyes
seem kind, gentle. Chestnut brown. She goes out because
she likes music, to avoid the young, overbearing landlord
who is always at her door to talk. Antoine knew such men.
Arrivistes, he said. She goes out in search of the man who will
listen, understand, even if she does not know why she needs
to tell her story. It has to be a man.

Detroit, Indiana, Puerto Rico, Connecticut, Nevis, Vermont.
Education, job, career. More education, another career, more
jobs. One night at dinner in Nevis, waves breaking softly on the
shore not more than a few feet away, Evelyn said my husband
doesn't touch me anymore. He's always tired. I tell myself he
works hard. He loves his children. He wants to support us well.
But I'm not young anymore. I know men like younger women.
Her look a question he could not answer, and she looked
away. At Lake Champlain at dusk, Sandy leaned against
him. A flight of geese headed south. An orange-lavender sky
streaked with gray above the Adirondack mountains. A chill
in the air. Summer ending. If there is nothing more to life
than this, she said, this is more than enough. Life is a trip
cross country Paula said. You meet someone, fall in love, stay.
Say Rochester. You fall out of love, move on, meet someone
else. Say Cleveland. Life moves on. You drive farther west.
The trip ends. Better be with someone.

We'll be back in ten minutes the tenor sax says. He smiles. He is tall, thin, good-natured. The kind of boy a girl's mother would want her daughter to meet. At tables around them conversation picks up. A stout girl with dark auburn hair, a fleshy face and a loose, baggy sweater moves closer to a thin girl with a crew cut and nose ring. Did you see them last night? he hears her say. She was all over him. At a table behind their booth, a middle-aged man with a graying crew cut diagrams something on a napkin to four, tall athletic young men What do you think? he hears a voice behind him ask. I have to do something. From the kitchen there are sounds of glasses and dishes being bussed. The phone rings at the bar and the heavy-set manager picks it up. While she talks she fingers a necklace.

She looks over his shoulder, towards the plate glass window at the front of the restaurant. Her neck is long, slender, and her head tilted back to one side. She seems to be looking for something. The street is busy, and those who pass by may glance in, although most of the time they hurry by without looking. Down the street to dinner, a movie, friends, lovers, home. Her eyes are large in her head, her look fixed. For a moment she frowns and bites her lip. She looks down and smiles, as if something has amused her. Her lips move while she runs a finger around the lip of the wineglass. Once again she looks out the window and he follows her eyes as they follow someone go by.

It had not turned out as she thought. What was she to do after Antoine left? Her uncle loaned her money for night classes and he got her work in a department store, but she did not have enough money to buy the right clothes for the job and they let her go. One day she saw some women standing on a corner of a cul-de-sac off St. Catherine and asked herself why they stood there in the middle of the day, not talking to anyone. Women who looked like her. Housewives shopping downtown. Salesclerks on lunch break. A man in a car said something to one of them and she got in his car. She would not do that. They might not have any other choice, but if she had no choice, she would not do it. You're fooling yourself she tells herself late at night in bed.

Beneath a cloudless sky. That's what everyone told him Puerto Rico would be like. Sun hot enough to dissipate the numbing cold of the north. But for months the time he was in Puerto Rico the sky would cloud over, darken several times a day, rain would follow, sometimes a few scattered drops, as if the sky spit, and every now and then a torrential downpour that noisily pounded tin roofs. During the rainy season he watched sheets of rain whip across the street from his office. He had been caught out more than once during a downpour. It was impossible not to avoid during rainy season and sometimes there were no stores to pop into until the rain passed and, in any event, the rain might not stop for hours. He would return home drenched, ice-cold, chilled he felt as he had not been chilled before. He had no hot water after eight in the morning and could not shower to warm himself up. He would wrap himself in a blanket and lie on the couch. You want cloudless skies, endless brilliant blue overhead, sun brightening days. You forget the details.

If the music speaks to you, takes you by the hand, you follow it without looking back. You do not ask where. One moment follows another, as if it were meant to be. You cross a meadow, fragrance of spring wheat in the air, stop at a pond with lavender day-lilies on its surface. She leans against your shoulder and takes your hand. A hummingbird hovers by fuschia nearby. She shakes her head and rubs her cheek against yours. Her silken hair a caress. The music touches you lightly on the shoulder. Time to move on.

The middle-aged man with a crew cut and the four young men have left. Two boys have joined the girls at the table.

One is thin with long, straight black hair, a Fu-Manchu moustache. The other is blond, well-built, and kisses each girl on the cheek. At the end of the bar, a balding man with long, stringy hair and ears that stick out sits hunched over a beer. At the other end of the bar, the chef and manager talk quietly. The waitress stands in front of him and asks if he wants another beer. She is tall, slim, and her white blouse is unbuttoned two or three buttons, her black skirt short and tight. She smiles. Her hair is in dreadlocks and her lipstick bright coral. She is full of the confidence of youth and tells her friends her job is less a job than a social life. The people she meets. You would not believe what some evenings are like. Yes, he nods to the waitress, restless. He turns to the woman at the next table and she looks at him, as if she is about to say something. "Welcome back," the tenor sax says. "We have some new music we want to play."

She leans back in her chair, head back, shuts her eyes. Her lips open slightly. The side of her face is shadowy, dark, but her lips are distinct, luminous under dimmed lights. The day she stood outside the white slat fence of the *dacha*. Leaves covered grass, but underneath a large window with broken panes at the side of the house white and lavender lilacs bloomed. The branches of an elm in front swayed softly in a breeze. Why do you want to see it? her mother asked. When your grandfather died in 1917, we left it empty. For awhile some Bolshevik troops stayed there. Then some government officials. I don't remember the last time anyone lived in it. Her mother wiped her forehead with a handkerchief. By the time you are my age it will have collapsed. Several years later she took Sergei to the *dacha* and they explored it room by room. In her grandparents' bedroom, he touched her lips his fingers, unbuttoned her blouse. For a moment he put a finger against his lips. Quiet, he said. We don't want your *stada baba* to hear. His lips brushed hers and moved up to kiss her closed eyes. She felt as if she were on the edge of a precipice. For a moment she touches her cheek before she opens her eyes, smiles, as if apologetic, to the man sitting at the table next to hers.

She looks down. Her eyes are deep-set under her brows, in shadow. Several curly locks of hair have fallen onto her forehead. Her hands are folded in her lap. She has crossed her legs and swings one leg back and forth. Her face a mask. The difficulties Sergei faced. The expectations his family placed on him. He would never free himself of them. For a moment the man sitting at the next table leans back in his chair and rubs his bald head. Some evenings he has to drink one beer after another before the battle that rages in his head ends. He hunches over his beer. They can't take that away from him. He knows how to stop things, even if the battle is never won. He raises his Labatt's to his lips. He may win a battle but never the war.

Some evenings he goes to a bar in his small town in Vermont. The town shuts down early, and the video stores are busy, but this bar draws in those the night spits out. Some of those he sees at the bar were there 20 years ago. The rest are young, not married, and they need alcohol and talk to make them feel alive, need the music to keep from breaking out. How else do they survive? The train leaves on a regular schedule. The one to take them to the inevitable, uncertain future they will recognize later as their lives. They see those at the bar who have refused the future or been rejected by it, and know that it is no future, no future at all. Pump up the volume. Fuck it. Louder. Let's hear it. It does not matter what, as long as it is fast, loud, shuts everything else out.

You like jazz? he asks. She smiles, enigmatic, and turns her chair in his direction to face him, and waits for him to say something more, as if he had not asked her a question For a moment he looks down at his beer before he asks, You come here often? I like music, she says. All kinds of music. She runs a hand along the edge of the table. Sometimes I check the paper for the listings. She crosses her legs, swish of nylon against nylon a whisper. Sometimes I just choose a part of the city I'd like to be in for the evening. Her hand has stopped moving back and forth along the edge of the table and she looks down to examine her nails. There's always music somewhere in Montreal'. Her pale green eyes examine him.

His eyes meet hers, but in a moment he looks away. The jazz trio has joined their friends in a booth. At the door an older white-haired couple with florid faces ask the manager if they are still serving food. The scrawny, balding guy at the bar still sits hunched over his beer, his glass full, and he does not know if it is another beer or the same one. He gives the woman a smile, massages a tight shoulder. It does not seem to be difficult. Everywhere he looks he sees couples. Sees them walk down the street together. Talk, laugh, smile. Enter stores, restaurants, theaters. He picks up the napkin and re-folds it. She sits by herself. He sits by himself. A lot of people in this world sit by themselves. Once again he takes his napkin and wipes his hands with it. This fall he said to Peter, I need a woman to complete myself. I know how that sounds. Women have heard that story before. He laughs. They're tired of men wanting to be saved. They don't want to be seen as some sort of cosmic last resort. He shrugged his shoulders. It must be tough to be Helen of Troy. He peels some of the Labatt's label off. I don't know, he says. I'm not Canadian.

Momentarily she frowns, bites her lip. Yesterday she saw Antoine at the corner of St. Laurent and St. Catherine and followed him into the Complexe Desjardins. He went into a woman's store. For a moment she rubs her forehead. As if she is one of those women who can't let go of their men, so pitiful their love is. She's attractive he thinks. Really striking. Those prominent, sharp cheekbones, small, perfectly-formed lips. Why is she alone? If she were waiting for someone, he would have been here by now. She shakes her head. The moment she saw Antoine cross the street her heart beat faster and her face got hot. A spasm grips her stomach. She smiles at the man at the table next to hers. Sergei was the romance of her youth. Antoine was a man. Where are you from? she asks. She waves a hand in front of her to take in the restaurant, as if to say everyone here is from somewhere else. At least she had not gone to bed with Antoine when he asked.

He has come to Montreal for the weekend and did not feel like going to the film he had planned to see. It's not an easy film to see friends told him and he was not sure he was up for it. Tonight she wanted to be in this part of the city. She saw the restaurant had jazz. Each of them finding their way as they found their way. Nomads in a world nomads have no place. Vagabonds of the night. Too many days counting the hours. Too many nights alone. Too many years somewhere else. They come in from the cold, but have spent too much time in airport terminals, train stations, bus depots, and it never works. Don't you understand? everyone tells them. Don't you get it? I need something else they say. Do I want to live as others live? Yes, she says every night, and then, no. Yes, he says, but it's not me. Vermont, he says. I'm from Vermont.

See you next Friday, the tenor sax says. Thanks for coming out. Weren't they good? she asks. They're young. But I think they have talent. His dark chestnut eyes gleam. He imagines his fingers tracing the shape of her lips. Last week I heard African music for the first time, she says. In Laval. She leans forward and puts her hands on the back of the other chair at his table. I'm Russian, and there's no Russian music in Montreal. Years ago I went to the Troika Restaurant. Do you know it? It's on Crescent. *Tres cher*. Ironically she smiles. A man in a red jacket comes to your table with a balalaika and sings. That's not music.

Yes. I've been to the Troika, he says. Her glance is sharp. Anyone who has been to the Troika did not stay at this hotel. Years ago. He had gone with his wife on a summer vacation through eastern Canada. They had been to the Pontchartrain in Detroit, but never any place like the Troika. An Australian sat with a Japanese on one side of them. An Egyptian with a Latvian on the other. At one point he smiled at his wife, shrugged his shoulders. My mother would never eat at the Troika. She would look at the menu and say soup costs more than a meal at home. They knew no French, and their waiter was brusque, perfunctory. The woman leaned forward, her arms on the table, waiting for him to continue. Yes, he says and nods. The man with a balalaika came by. You're right. He wasn't any good. He wouldn't leave until we tipped him. We must not have tipped him well. He looked at us, as if we should not be in the restaurant, and muttered something about Americans. My wife shook her head, laughed. Welcome to Canada.

You're divorced? she asks. Yes. Years ago. You? Yes. Like you. Divorced years ago. Do you miss it? he asks. She looks away and he notices a pulse in her neck. Sorry, he says. I don't mean to pry. Her fingers pick at threads of her pale blue sweater. She brushes hair off her forehead and looks at him intently. I just got fired from my job, she says. My supervisor always put his arm on my shoulder when he told me what to do. I felt his glance on me when I went to the photocopier. You've got nice legs, he said. You should wear short skirts more often. Her fingers pick at threads of her sweater. She leans back, crosses her legs, seems to be thinking of something. Last week he had a hand on my shoulder, she says, and while he talked about how he wanted the Excel spread sheet done, he touched me. Stop, I told him. Don't do that. I was over-reacting, he said. She took a sip of wine. At the end of the day, he came to my desk and said, Friday will be your last day. Have your desk cleaned out. Your check will be in the mail. Her green eyes, flecked with gray, smoldering. For a moment she looked down at her hands clasped on the table. When I look at you, she says to the man across from her, you look back. He did not even look in my direction when he told me I was fired.

Her lids droop, as if she is resting, her eyes blank. She wets her lips with her tongue. Dark lavender of her lids. Momentarily her nostrils flare. In the nineteenth century police and scientists used photographs to identify criminals and the insane. But if her character is written on her face, he cannot read it. Her Slavic cheeks, pale green eyes, and small, perfectly-formed lips tell him no more than there is beauty in the world and we seek it out wherever it might be.

I didn't care for the job anyway, she says. For a moment she wets her lips with her tongue. It paid the bills while I finished my degree. She presses her lips together tightly. What did you study? he asks. She leans forward, her eyes still in shadows. He fingers the wool at the neck of his sweater. Computer science, she says. I'm going to be a web designer. You lose me there, he says. I find the phone too complicated. In calculus. He drinks from his Labatt's. I took a course. In calculus all problems begin with the obvious. What everyone agrees to be true. Wryly he smiles. The obvious was never obvious to me.

She was not dumb. She saw how machines were replaced and upgraded in offices on a regular basis, how those who understood them got promoted, how those who did not were let go. Technology was on everyone's lips. At first she took night classes to help her get better jobs, earn more money. Computers were progress. The wave of the future. One of her professors, a stooped man whose shirt was always out of his pants and tie loosened, cautioned them. Understand this, he said. You'll learn skills that will help you get better jobs, but you'll never be in charge. You're just foremen in the age of technology. Unless you're a damn good hacker, that is. Foreman would not be bad she thought. She did not expect she would be anything more than proficient, capable. We need to know how to use computers, she says, just as we have to know how to drive and use the phone. An ATM machine would confuse my mother. She smiles and for a moment her nose wrinkles. He notices a minute dark smudge on the bridge of her nose.

Divorce is difficult, he says. You have to look in the mirror and you may not like what you see. It is hard, she says. The man I fell in love with and married just after I arrived in Montreal still wants to see me. She runs fingers across her temples. For a moment she looks across the restaurant in the direction of the bar. She looks tired. He's remarried and has three children. Our first love is different, he replies. Sometimes we carry it all our lives. I don't know, she says. Love is one thing. Marriage another. I was not the right woman for him to marry. Abruptly he laughs. Everyone talks about the right one. He rubs his chin. Most of us settle for what we can have. Is that why we're divorced? she asks. We wouldn't settle for less? Her smile is sour and she looks away, her lips barely moving. We must be stupid.

He knows that the jazz trio has joined their friends at the booth to his left. The older couple has come in, taken a table, ordered dinner. The manager stands next to the cash register, leans back against the bar to rest her feet, smokes a cigarette. The waitress asks the students if they want another round. The balding guy at the bar? He's still there. He pays them no attention while he follows her fingers trace lines and curves on the tablecloth, touches the silver pendant on her earring. Her fingers are long with silver-blue nails. Her ear is curved gently like a shell. Her skin is smooth, unwrinkled. I came in here tonight he thinks because I had to get out of my room, could not be in Montreal and do nothing. Weariness weighed on him. He had a hard week at work and had to get out of town, but nothing in Montreal drew him to it. He was distracted, bored, disappointed. He was not even aware of her at the next table when he sat down.

She leans forward, pulls the other chair at his table towards her, puts her elbows on it, clasps her hands together against her forehead. Inside the triangle her arms make, he can see her nose, mouth, chin, but not her eyes, which her arms obscure. She waits for him to say something. There is no urgency. He will say something. She will answer. She will say something. He will answer. She can read his eyes, see him frown, laugh, massage his bald head. He can only see her smile, laugh, grimace, bite her lips. He raises his hands in front of him in mock supplication. Yes, he says. I think we are stupid. Every damn one of us. His eyebrows go up and his lip curls down. Sometimes stupidity is exactly what we need.

His gaze remains fixed on her lips and teeth. Not that he wants to kiss her, feel her lips against his. He does he realizes, but to see her this way changes how he sees her and he cannot look away. As after love, your bodies wrapped around one another, your left arm embracing her, all you see is the nape of her neck, the slope of her shoulder and you notice short, curly hairs high on her neck, darker than the hair of her head. You examine a pale white scar on her shoulder, no more than half an inch. You note a minute rust-brown mole on her back you had not seen before. She is no longer the woman you know. At this moment you trace the scar with a finger.

His eyes look quizzical, large, behind his glasses. Tiny red veins crisscross his nose. For a moment he fingers his earring. His look is serious, intent. She has learned to distrust her instincts. What did her mother say about high foreheads? Before he became bald his forehead must have been high. At one point she read astrology and asked those she met what their astrological signs were. One Sunday after Antoine left, she found herself in church. At first, it was little more than part of a weekly routine, like shopping or laundry. Something to do Sunday mornings, rather than lie in bed. One Tuesday evening she found herself kneeling in a pew in church, hands folded on the back of the bench in front of her, asking God for advice. She always knows when a man is honest, but she never knows if she can trust him. His lips are thick and there is a gap in his upper teeth. His moustache makes him look fierce, but she cannot imagine he is.

Broadly she smiles. Her left cheek twitches. She waits. There is a slight indentation in the middle of her upper lip, and a line runs from it to the end of her nose. The skin of her lower lip is cracked. He still cannot see her eyes and her face inside her arms is a mask. For a moment her lips tremble. He must be the one to say something. He must be the one to take the next step. She came to the restaurant for music. She has had good talk. She stays there.

The night joy lifted him. The day loss devastated him. The moment satisfaction was recalled. There was a song on the radio, the final notes of a concerto, glass shattering, a film soundtrack, the incessant, jarring rhythm of a pile driver. It was the last week of the year, unseasonably cold. It was the Fourth of July at a parade. The fall there was a minor quake. One night he played the song over and over. Dylan and Johnny Cash. Girl From the North Country. Then he forgot. It was gone. One night driving home he hears the song again, if only a word or two, a guitar riff, and that night of joy, day of loss, moment of satisfaction is back, as if time had stopped.

He runs a thumb across his moustache, rubs the back of his head. His eyes are dark, hooded. Watch a man's hands her mother told her. You'll know how he'll treat you from what he does with them. See how long his fingers are. Her mother laughed. Like his feet. You need to know that. For her it is not the hands, but the eyes. He has a strong jaw, an aquiline nose, a high forehead, but she learns nothing from them. She can get lost in eyes. Of course, she knows what's in men's eyes. Their eyes have undressed her. But she pays attention to how their eyes flicker and glint, their color vary, blankness be pulled down like a shade. How they shrink to a pinpoint. For a moment her mind drifts back in time, Antoine, the night he left, but she puts the memory aside. It can wrap itself around her and make her crazy, even if some nights in bed she embraces its delirium. She examines him. Dark chestnut eyes, flecked with gold. A light in them.

His eyes on her lips. Hers upon his eyes. What can he understand from her lips? His eyes speak for him she thinks. She moves the chair closer, her arms still resting on its back, her face still enclosed by her arms.. His fingers pick at the Labatt's label. Every man in her life might have been the same man he thinks. The wrong man. He does not care. He waits for the moment to say something, but he knows what it will be. It will come when it comes. There is no hurry.

You want to hear more music? he asks. It's not far. You probably know the place. Her face inside the triangle of her arms has begun to distract him. He cannot see her eyes. He speaks to her as he might a priest. For a moment she rubs her cheek against her arm. The Café Sarajevo, he says. They play Slavic music. She lowers her head and he sees her eyes before she straightens. Gypsy music. The last time he was there everyone was up dancing after two in the morning. Several women jumped on tables. The guttural voice of the singer driving them, violins frenzied. Her eyes are cloudy, unredeemed. It's a small place, he says. It's always full. A Serb exile owns it.

Some have come to the Café Sarajevo for the first time. A friend had said something. *Mirror* had a comment. They would not be back. The music was too melancholy and slow or too frenzied, driven. Those who come back come in, nod to one another. They don't miss a Friday. The waitress asks how they've been, how was work, are the children all right. For a moment he removes his glasses and cleans them. Sorry, he says. I was thinking of something. She smiles, her white teeth luminous in the shadows the triangle her arms have caused. I can't say the music has much melody, he says. Its rhythm follows how the band feels. So. He holds out his left hand and drops it. Sometimes fast, he says. Then he draws a circle with his right hand. Sometimes slow. He shrugs his shoulders. We can't find the words for what moves inside us he thinks. We fall back on music, song. That's why they come Friday after Friday, their nod to one another acknowledgment. How can I say what it is, he says. Something like Slavic soul.

At the Café Sarajevo the violinist moved close to the lone dancer, brought his violin near her face. Slowly they move, the woman leading and the violin following and then the violin leading and the woman following. As if the woman were as much the music as the violin and each, in turn, took the lead from one another. Her arms describe arcs, arabesques, geometries. They explore the space in front of her, reaching out, tentative, pausing, turning, finding direction, hesitant, an aimlessness waiting to find itself, search without goal. As if her hands need to touch the space in front of her, hold it, know it as she knows a lover's body. The singer clasps his hands together, picks the beat up, his voice rising. The violinist bows furiously. The woman stamps her feet, throws her arms about wildly, a dervish possessed.

She leans her head against the back of the booth, her eyes

shut. For a moment she runs a finger across her forehead. Her lips move. The violins pick the beat up, the singer cradles the microphone. Several women are dancing. At the bar, the raven-haired bartender in a tight, black sheath dress with a string of pearls around her neck talks to several men. He turns back to her. She pushes her head against the back of the booth and her head tilts to one side. Her jaw is slack, listless. One hand rests on a thigh. A smile crosses her lips. Is it memories of another night, another band, another man? The music taken her by the hand, led her to a dream she has dreamed more than once, let her play with its possibility? Once again she smiles and her cheeks dimple, as if she has read his mind. The music comes to an abrupt stop with the rapid screeching of violins, the strangled cry of the singer. She opens her eyes and looks at him for a moment, her eyes luminous, transparent. Then her eyes cloud over and there is a fixed smile on her face.

What is there to say? The band is good. No. She does not want to dance. She is content to sit and listen. What is there to say? She has come into a hotel bar to hear jazz, not expecting anything of the evening except for it to pass. He had come into a hotel bar to let the evening pull him through it. What is there to say? A man at a table alone. A woman at a table alone. A man and a woman talking. A man and a woman leaving together. They know this ebb and flow of things, have been there more evenings than they like to remember, but they have reached the place where they must do something or nothing. Move the evening forward or stop it. Few experiences in life cross a threshold and they don't know if this is one they want to cross. Every night sleep may take us into uncharted territory, but during the day there are consequences. When it comes down, it comes down hard and fast.

The arrows on the map come out of the East and point

west. Russia to Canada. Hungary to the States. Serbia to Montreal. So many following the fault-lines. Down one-way streets that cut through lives. Last month he had been at the Café Sarajevo when a woman came up to get beers. He had seen her and what he assumed to be her daughter come in. It'll be awhile, he told her. It's crowded and the bartender has her own guest list. They talked. Her daughter went to McGill and she had come across town for a parents' weekend. What McGill planned for the weekend, she said, could not be more numbing. So English. They never do anything without first tightening their sphincters. They had to get away. They went down Clark towards a place she knew had good jazz. Biddles. They looked in at the Café Sarajevo. What do you think? she said to her daughter. Why not?

Sometimes she shuts her eyes at the cinema and listens to the soundtrack. She can always tell when the end of the film is near. If a door shuts or a man enters the room, the music rises and you sat up, paid attention. Several minutes ago he looked at her with a question in his eyes. His forehead wrinkled and she noticed how loose the flesh was under his chin. Skin does not lie she thinks. She shuts her eyes. The music is loud, fast, driven, the harsh voice of the singer holding on to the music as it can, his voice swallowed by his throat.

When did it begin? She had been a child, maybe five years old. Whenever she saw the boy down the street, she got a funny feeling in her stomach, her cheeks turned red, her heart beat faster. She was struck dumb whenever she found herself in the same room with him. Sergei surprised her. He led her step by step, and she did not know she could be as happy, feel so good. She identified Antoine with Canada. He was a new world for her, surprising and exciting, if not, at times, threatening. She did not hold back. As if she had not known her body before, not know how a look could be a hand on her forehead, calming her. How he came across a room with a smile on his face. How he whispered into her ear. When he left for good, something had been torn out of her, and she had to get it back. There was the tall man. The thin man. The blue-eyed man. The one who stuttered. The one whose breath was bad. The man who would be love.

They go up Clark to Sherbrooke, his arm around her shoulder. Her hand brushes his hip. His hand feels how soft her arm is under the thin cloth of her coat. She leans her head against his shoulder. That was nice, he says. Yes, she answers. Yes it was. It was a good evening. At the corner of Sherbrooke, he reaches for her hand and after a moment's hesitation, she gives it to him. For a moment he looks down Sherbrooke towards St. Laurent and then searches her face. I hate to end the evening, he says. Don't, she says, and squeezes his hand before she removes hers. Which way is your hotel? she asks. West. Down Sherbrooke, he answers. I go the other way, she says. She smiles and he imagines how her lips would feel against his, her tongue touch his ear. It was a nice evening, she says. Let it go at that.

There is a chill in the air, and he tucks his chin down on his leather jacket, but he is sweating, his forehead pounds. He has drunk too much and is not getting any younger. His body can't take it anymore. His legs are stiff, sore, tired from a hard run up Mount Royal before dinner. The hotel is only two, three blocks down Sherbrooke. He picks a stone off the pavement and flings it across a vacant lot. Overhead, the moon slides out from behind a cloud. Down the street, an old couple argue at the corner of Rue Parc. He is stooped, pulls away from her. She is heavy, and her chin has folds of flesh under it. Both of them carry plastic shopping bags. Their harsh, angry voices carry down the street to him. He feels a hand take his arm. She looks at him, bright scarlet lips held tightly together and then she smiles. Don't misunderstand, she says. We say good-bye in the morning.

Her face floats across a lunar landscape and he reaches out to capture the apparition, but before he can do so, it disappears, her good-bye kiss thrown across a chasm, haunting. At the horizon, her pale green eyes gleam in a dark sky. Restless, hungry eyes that dart back and forth, like a bird approaching, retreating quickly, stopping, edging closer, circling. In front of him, not more than a foot away, they vanish. Her face pops up to his left, is replaced by another, a third, a series of faces, each with a different expression, like masks put on and taken off. Her lips glow in front of him, come close, smile, frown, tease, trace an artery in his neck, nuzzle an ear, wet his eyelids before they are against his lips swallowing him. His leg jerks and he wakes. For a moment he rubs his eyes before he rolls onto his side. She lies on her back, her breath rising and falling slowly in her body. Her lipstick is smudged, hair pasted against her forehead, a dark red abrasion on her neck. Suddenly her nostrils flare and her nose wrinkles, as if she is about to sneeze. He props himself up on an elbow to look at her more closely. This woman who moved against him just minutes ago, breathing heavily, eyes closed, silent, brushing hair off her forehead, steadying herself with a hand, pulling him closer, her breath harsh, labored, mouth open, rubbing her face against his shoulder. He touches the bone of her cheeks, the delicate skin of her lips, the long line of her neck. In the morning they will say little, not look at one another, dress quickly. For the moment they have one another. This place, then.

II

The story told itself, but was not in its telling. Chris had gone to Montreal, met Tania at a bar, and they spent the night together. Before she left the next morning, she turned to him at the door of his room in the hotel, her hand on the door knob, the hint of a smile on her face. Take care of yourself, she said, and looked at him closely, her pale green, transparent eyes dark. It was good. When Chris moved towards her, she held up a hand. Don't, she said. And was gone.

Chris puts on Sinead O'Connor. Her voice plaintive, defiant before it sinks only to rise again like a phoenix. "I will meet you in somebody's office," O'Connor says. Chris leans back against the armchair and rubs his eyes. He takes a sip of bourbon. "I'll talk but you won't listen to me." Up to the edge, the drop precipitous. "I know what your answer will be." Raw, laid waste. Driven towards the only silence that will speak.

He was certain he saw Tania last week on Main Street. For a moment the woman glanced at him, as if she knew him. She wore tight levis, a leather jacket, boots with heels. Even as he knew it could not be her, he turned to follow her. She was already halfway down the block, and by the time he reached the alley to the craft center, she had disappeared. He glanced into the restaurant by the creek, looked across the pedestrian bridge.

Chris puts on P. J. Harvey. Her voice angry, loathing. Nails raked across flesh. "How to walk. Where to run," insinuates itself as a reproach. For years life had pushed Chris along. Everywhere he stopped not a stopping point. Everywhere he went not a destination. The guitar relentless. Her voice blistered, abandoned. And then, cut off.

Tonight it is Vermont. Yesterday Connecticut. The day before. Chris leans back against the armchair. Puerto Rico, Detroit, Indiana, Detroit. His knees ached. One calf was sore. His first job in high school had been washing cars. The first days he would look at the clock after he finished a car and see that only a few minutes had passed. He did not think he would make it to the end of the day.

Two strangers meet one night in Montreal. They spend the night together. The next morning they leave without saying anything. Silenced by a past that prevented them living in the present. "If you do not. Cannot," he hears Harvey. Her voice judgment. The silence Harvey hears. Her guitar ripping the scab off.

Chris, he hears Tania ask, what are we going to do tonight? The sound of her voice brings her forth in his mind. Her smile enigmatic. She leans back against the table. She is wearing levis, a soft white shirt unbuttoned at the neck, an Indian bead necklace. Her skin is dark against the luminous white of her shirt. Who was that? she asks. The woman in his mind more real than the one in Montreal could ever be. For a moment he concentrates on the lavender and coral beads of her necklace.

He seems to have pressed fast-forward on his life since he'd been back from Montreal. Tania came to him in the middle of the night and when he reached for her, his hand waved at air. He would turn on the street when he heard her laugh but there would be no one there. He felt her glance upon him when he was alone. P. J. Harvey, he says as if he were talking to someone. His glasses glint in the light of the lamp next to the couch.

He remembers Tania's deep-set eyes hooded under her eyebrows. He sees her lean back against a table, rock back and forth on her heels. Broadly she will smile, teeth brilliant white, perfect. I see the look in your eyes, she says. He sees her pick up the P. J. Harvey cd and examine the photo of Harvey on the cover. I want you, she says, putting the cd down and looking at him intently. Her left cheek twitches and her forehead wrinkles. Her nostrils flare. She drops her head.

Last night Chris dreamt he saw her stop in the middle of the bridge over Otter Creek, her gaze on the falls below the Main Street viaduct, bats circling back and forth above the water. He waved, but she did not see him. Tania, he said, but she did not turn. When he got closer, he saw that tears streaked the cheeks of a woman who was not Tania.

He see himself lower his face to hers. She shivers when he kisses her and her lips part. Her body presses against his. He cradles the back of her head with a hand, runs a hand through her hair. Her hair silken, a scent of lilac about her, the urgency of her tongue.

He wakes on the couch, one arm stiff from having slept on it, his eyes unfocussed. The cd player still on. He closes the book he had been reading when he fell asleep and puts it on the floor. His face is ruddy, wrinkled. For weeks Tania materialized in his life though he knew she could not be there. For weeks he brought her forth. The woman who one day had been there was no longer there. She was never there. He pulls a woolen blanket up over his chest.

...

Tania wakes. For months she rolled over in bed in the morning, uneasy, not sure how far the landlord would go. More than once he knocked at the door late at night. I apologize, he would say. I smelled smoke. The woman below says a pipe is leaking. You told me your radiator does not work. He would look around the bedroom for signs of a man, ask inane questions. He refused to believe she was not interested in him. No was not a word women could say.

This morning she brings Chris into the room. His smile is kind, gentle, cheeks dimpled, shaved head gleaming. His chestnut-brown eyes are large through rimless glasses. Lazily she stretches her legs and reaches for the head board behind her. Chris, she says. The thin light of morning sun shimmers against the pane and outlines him against it, bronze particles of dust rising and falling around him. His body dark against the window.

For a moment she frowns, bites her lip. Her forehead creases. When she arrived in Canada, she found herself thinking of Sergei while she interviewed for a job. I'm sorry, she said more than once. What did you say? Later, weeks later, after Antoine left her, she walked the streets around his office, hoping to see him. Why do you hang on to Robert? her therapist asked. You thought of Antoine for months. You think of him today. He leaned back in his chair, tapped a pen against the desk.

You don't let men go. Even Sergei. He lifted the pen and sighted down it. A teenager. A boy. On the subway, Tania heard a woman advise a friend to have more than one man in her life. If one leaves, she said, you'll still have the other one. Who isn't alone? she answered the therapist.

When she slips into sleep at night, harsh, incomprehensible dreams keep her riveted, her body rigid, fearful, until she has to pull herself up from sleep to escape them, saying, no, don't do that. Saying yes, do what you want. Saying stay. Just stay.

One scene plays itself over and over. Antoine pulls his trousers up, wipes his brow. His face is dark, angry, and he does not look at her. She does not give him space, he says. She's in his face all the time. For a moment something he sees through the bay window catches his attention. Her lips tremble. There is a sinking feeling in the pit of her stomach.

He has said it before. Said it too many times. She won't let him breathe.

She pushes this scene away and seizes hold of a memory of Antoine approaching the bed, naked, his chest matted with thick, dark-black hair, a slight paunch she kidded him about. There is desire in his eyes, certainty in his step. She props herself up on an elbow, leans forward and touches his penis. My girl, he says. My good girl.

We say good-bye in the morning, she told Chris. The night was a gift. She ran a hand down his shoulder, her fingers shy. That it was she thinks. Let's not fool ourselves, she added. It was what it was. Nothing more. His fingers touched her cheeks, ran down her nose, traced, ever so gently, her lips. Close your eyes, he said. I want you to feel my lips with your body. Nothing less. She does not know how long they stayed in the same time even though she knew that their time was not theirs. When she first saw Chris she knew it was not possible, but. There was always but.

...

Had Chris been drinking the night he listened to P. J. Harvey and saw Tania in the room? Had he gone without sleep the night he remembered they had walked down to the creek and saw a beaver slap water with his tail once it became aware of them? He was not drunk. Was Tania a hallucination? He does not have them.

What is speaks for itself.

What is not speaks for itself.

He gets up and goes into the kitchen, drinks a glass of water, leans back against the counter. He should do something with the linoleum floor. The landlord said he would take something off the rent if Chris did. His mother always made a schedule of what needed to be done. His father avoided it as much as he could. He would rather play golf, go to the poolroom, drink with his buddies. She would have finished the floor by now.

He sided with his father, but his mother was right. If you did not do what needed to be done, no one would do it for you. He takes his glasses off and rubs his eyes. He would not be a slave to his work, his apartment, the daily round. But if he were not, he could not live as he did.

Tonight he had to complete a report on admission policies. The committee wants it by the end of the week, the Dean said this afternoon. It would not be difficult. Just take time. Numbing, deadening time. At one point last night while he worked on the report, he felt Tania touch his shoulder.

What's this, Chris? he hears her ask. For a moment he thought of his father, who let himself settle in the traces when he wanted to dance the night away. He thought of how Tania's hand on his thigh would feel. A woman who could not be here had taken over his life.

Outside, pale gray clouds obscure the moon. Chris can barely see the birches down by the tracks near the water. Across the creek, there is a light in a top floor window of an apartment and shimmering, luminous ripples in the water reflect light from the restaurant next to the apartment. Suddenly a late March wind springs up and the branches of trees twist and turn, sharp cracks of branches snapping.

...

Near Tania in the bar, a man in levis, blue work shirt and denim jacket sits at a table with a woman in a black skirt and pale lavender silk blouse buttoned to the neck. His face is dark, as if he has not shaved. Her forehead wrinkles and she bites her lips. Behind them, the bartender dries glasses with a towel and puts them under the counter. The woman has prominent cheekbones, thin, delicate lips, curly sandy-brown hair cut short.

Tania feels a hand press against her shoulder. Look at them, a voice says. They are lovers, but he is tired of her. He wants to end it. She feels she'll die if he does. She'll kill herself. She has told him she will. See how her hand reaches out for his. He won't take it. He'll turn away. She will look at him as if for the last time. Look at how they kiss. His kiss tells her he needs to get away. Hers that he remember her. It always ends the same way. His hand tightens on Tania's shoulder.

_____ the woman pleads. It's over, the man answers. She takes a step towards him. He pushes her away. She tugs at his arm. He shrugs her hand off. No, she cries out. Stay. For a moment he looks at her, his lip curled down, dismissive, before he turns away. _____ she says, and puts her arms around him, presses her breasts against his back. He takes her hands and thrusts them away from him. _____ she whispers, _____ almost indistinct, as he walks away from her.

He turns at the door, his face dark, eyes deep-set in his head. She takes a step towards him. She cannot understand why he wants to leave her. No one will love him as she does. He must see that. She hears the shot before she sees the gun in his hand and black and white square tiles of the floor rush up to her before she loses consciousness. Blood spreads across her pale lavender blouse, her head turned to the side, her mouth slack.

_____ looks at the body on the floor for a long moment before he comes back, lies down next to her, cradles her head against his chest. It will be all right, he says. It's over. A sob escapes him. It could not be any other way. He strokes her hair. I could not live with you, he continues. I wished you were dead. I am, she says. He buries his head against her breast. I can't live without you, he says, his voice no more than a whisper. Her scream is long, drawn-out, harsh, as if only death can release it.

The man you met, she hears the voice behind her. Chris is his name, right? You think it will be any different with him? When will you learn? You want love. You fool yourself. The moment you put your arms around the one you love, feel his soft breath on your neck, you find yourself more alone than you've ever been. We want someone to hold. We hold only ourselves. Tania turns away, gulps down wine. She wipes her brow and leans back. Her face hot, wet. Don't you ever learn? You remember how you put your arm around Sergei under the elm in front of the *dacha*, your head on his shoulder. You call the wind through the trees back.

She pulls away. Her back ramrod-stiff. Her head high. Her lavender blouse has pulled out of her skirt, the elastic of her coral underwear visible, a navy blue *fleur-de-lis* tattooed on her lower back, her skin unsettling in its nakedness.

...

Chris has lived in this town for years, knows its people, their stories. For years he listened to friends explain their lives. Why what happened did. You know why she left him? Calhoun would ask. She reached the point where if she did not. It was just, Harper would add. You don't know his family. Chris said nothing. He never got beyond who, when, where. He mastered the art of leaning against walls.

One night in the Adirondacks with Diane he followed a road the map said would take them to Port Henry. It curled higher into mountains and narrowed to not much more than a path, pavement becoming stone, stone gravel, gravel dirt. There must be logging trucks on this road he thought. It must go through. At one point they saw an elderly couple walking down the road ahead of them and Chris stopped to ask them where the road went and whether it was possible to go farther.

You won't get through, they said. Chris guessed he would have to back down a winding road perhaps for as long as a quarter mile before he could turn the car around. We've come this far, he said to Diane. We can't go back now. They waved to the couple and edged forward.

In a half mile they came to a cross road not much wider than the road they were on. At least it was paved. Two miles later they came to Route 9N, just outside Elizabethtown. When he had said, let's go on, he thought Diane never looked so beautiful, smoky-blue eyes, the beginning of a smile on a face touched by moonlight. She brushed blonde hair back. Do we have a choice? she had asked. Why was a road that did not go anywhere but did.

What's going on? Dan asks. Yesterday when Jennifer asked what you thought of Clark's talk, you said you had been thinking of something else. You knock down bourbon. Before Beal gets a drink for someone else, you're pointing to your empty glass. Gayle asked me the other day if there was anything going on in your life. Your work has slipped, she said.

His father knew it was never a good thing to say anything at work. Whatever he might say drew attention to him. You did not want that. The foreman knew there was always a reason a worker kept his mouth shut, but if he did not say anything, he could not do anything about it.. As long as the work got done. His father played the deadly game of the workplace. He kept to his machine.

Why don't you speak up? mother complained to father. You work hard. You should have got that promotion. Not Wagner. You said he kisses ass whenever he can. He only looked at her. When she said she had not married a man who would not go after it, he turned away. Chris never understood whether his father's silence was, in some way, refusal, protest. He turned away from mother Chris thought because there was nothing to say about what could not be said.

…

This longing. This bitter joy. Tania examines the deep red nails of her fingers. There was a certain solace in an overcast day. As if the indifferent universe at moments paused. For a moment she looks at the Impressionist landscape she has put above her couch. Two peasant women pause from their work and talk to one another. Behind them a granular, silver streak of smoke from a train pastes itself against the sky above woods. She hears the phone and does not know how long it has been ringing. For a moment she listens, unsure whether to let it ring or pick it up.

I want to see you, Antoine says. Her chest tightens and she brushes hair off her forehead. She has said yes, as if there were no other word. Until yes became the night that did not end. *You don't know what my life is like*, he continues. *Why I need you. Marriage is not what you think it is.* A shoulder to rest one's head on she thinks. Someone who does not leave. Who insists on nothing. It is gray wherever she looks. Gray. *You lose the passion.*

Last night she looked out on a full moon in a cold, clear winter sky. The dark alley alongside her apartment ghostly. She thought of Antoine asleep in bed with his wife, their youngest child whimper in sleep down the hall. If she let her hair grow, styled it differently, took advantage of its natural sheen. She hears a precipitous squealing of brakes, the crash of metal against metal, glass shatter, and then sudden, abrupt silence. *Antoine, you can't do this.*

After he left, she would lie on the bed, her knees tucked up against her breast, thighs still wet with his semen. It had gone on long enough. One evening she counted out sleeping pills. A white delivery truck apparently had taken the corner too fast, glanced off a navy blue Chevy, and flipped over. A heavy-set woman with a *babushka* tied on her head points towards the truck and cries for help. The driver had been thrown from the cab and pinned under the truck when it flipped over. *I can't take it anymore.* As if something had stopped, altered. Had wrapped itself around the unspoken.

A woman with a dish towel in her hands has come out of a brownstone near the truck. She gestures to the postman down the street. *I don't force you, Tania.* A crowd has gathered near the truck and several men try to lift the truck from the driver. They know it's useless. Antoine expected her to drop everything when he wanted to see her. A woman holds the driver's head and wipes his forehead with a cloth. Their evenings took them to an hour she could not believe possible. His heart slowed against her breast after they made love, his hand stroked hers. He would throw a leg across her thighs, tuck his head against her shoulder. They must have slept. *When you leave.*

One of the women by the truck has gone to the corner and looks up and down the street. Another woman kneels by the driver and wipes his brow. Surely, they must have slept. *I've got to go*, she says, her voice husky. The night she spent with Chris there had been no rush, their talk had gone where talk goes if it does not have to go anywhere. If the evening followed the dance of meeting, it also drifted like a walk in a park.

A woman near the truck raises her hands in supplication. A man turns away and rubs his eyes. The men at the truck stand and look at one another. One leans against the overturned truck, his head against its side. Another kneels by the driver and says something to him. She does not know anymore what is right and what wrong or if it made any difference. Whenever she thinks she has reached the right decision she fears it is the wrong one. *I've got to go,* she says, her voice husky. A woman near the truck raises her hands in supplication. A man turns away and rubs his eyes.

She wakes some mornings and finds Chris next to her, an arm thrown over the side of the bed, a hand on her thigh. He asks what she wants for breakfast, what they should do today. She wants to hold on to his voice, his soft laugh, the intensity of his gaze. She recalls the feel of the sheet on the hotel bed, the acrid taste of bourbon in his mouth. Some evenings dusk darkened the sky with her desire, and she never felt more desolate. Mornings she looked out from under blankets, calculating the possibilities of making it through another day.

...

Things go missing. Every time Chris puts a pen in his pocket, it's not there when he needs it. Yesterday he could not find one of his gloves. This winter he has lost one stocking cap, one calendar, three cds, and, for two days last week, his checkbook. How, he asked himself, could anyone lose a calendar? Last week he could not find a passage he had underlined in a book, even though he had looked at it fifteen minutes before.

Chris goes to the office. He takes a walk at noon. Do you want me to bring back coffee he asks before he leaves. He asks the clerk at the post office about her grandchildren. He stops at the bookstore to see if anything new has come in. Some days in winter a bitter wind causes his eyes to tear. He has done this for twenty years.

I knew you were not happy, the Dean said when he told her he was leaving. I didn't think you were stupid. She looked at him with pity, a touch of contempt, impatient to get back to her office.

We're never not on the clock, he says to Dan. For a moment he stirs coffee. Is that a way to live? Distractedly he shreds the plastic coffee stirrer. He appears tired, drawn. He takes his glasses off, cleans them with a napkin, and rubs his eyes before he puts them back on. In the first days of an 1830 revolution in France, a group of workers shot out clocks in Paris to stop the time that ruled their lives.

We've lost things. I don't want to say I can't get them back. For a moment Chris looks down at his hands on the table. The veins on the back of his hand are thick, pronounced, and the skin dark, wrinkled.

You remember Deb? One day she was there. The next day she was gone. She put her house on the market, packed her car, headed out of town, where she did not know. You worked with my mother, she said before she left. You know what her life was like. I was walking in her footsteps.

Chris counted them up. Those he has loved and those gone. The fierce determination of his mother. The love of his father. Amy, his wife. His close friends, the Martins. Catherine, who saw the two of them stand against the world. Tereza in a cast for months. Steve who put a plastic bag over his head one day and tied it off. The list was long.

For a moment he sees a dancer he had seen in the Café Sarajevo explore the space in front of her, reach out, tentative, turning, hesitant until the music took her over. There comes a moment if you don't do something, Chris says. He drains his coffee. I know it's hopeless.

***

It was less a story than a harsh, unredeemed fact. At eighteen she saw she was desirable and knew she would be loved. The world was there for the taking. This morning the mirror tells her that the skin of her neck has grown slack and for a moment she tugs loose skin. She looks to see if there are any white hairs in her sandy-brown hair. Some kind of mustard-yellow mucus cakes her lids. She should dye her hair. Her eyes would be striking with red hair. Yesterday she looked at a photo of herself arm-in-arm with Sergei in front of his family *dacha* in Russia. Her smile took in the world. Her face glowed. As if she could not be contained by the photograph. She was sixteen.

I won't be like mother, she told herself. Even then she saw how her father looked over her mother's shoulder and smiled at her cousin, Mila. Mila had the rosy skin of a farm girl and her breasts pushed against her blouse. She saw father smile at the neighbor's young wife. Everyone said the woman was too young for her husband and rolled their eyes. Her father had given her that look. One day. She does not remember how old she was. She had gone to her mother when her father looked at her that way and put her head against her shoulder.

A few years later she understood that father went out after whores while mother stayed at home and waited for him in bed. When he came home, he would turn his back to her in bed, the smell of a woman still on him. Last week the landlord stopped Tania on the stairs to say she had to leave. A friend of his needed a place. He would give her a month. She had not given in to him and he would not take that. He thinks I'm not young she thought. I should have been easy.

Last month she lay against Robert, who she had run into in the Eaton Center. He was engaged, but his fiancee was, all of a sudden, uncertain. Could he talk to her? The talk ended in a hotel bed. At the moment she came she did not know whether she had she been thinking of Antoine, how Robert tore her blouse when he took it off or how she touched herself in bed last night. Robert, she asked. When my thighs grow slack, the flesh hang loose, will you still want me?

His laugh was uneasy. He brought her hand around and

held it against his chest. You're a good-looking woman, Tania. Don't ever think you're not. It did not reassure her. Men cared only about their own desire. As long as they believe they have what it takes, it sets them up.

She smiles at herself in the mirror. Her lips without lipstick are a faded rust red, chapped. Lips men tell her they desire. A smile everyone likes. Pale green, transparent eyes, flecked with gray. Her forehead creases. Her looks have not made a life. For a moment she picks at something on her teeth with a fingernail.

You've been to places I never thought possible, her mother wrote. For all that, her life had not been much different. Tania knows what it feels like to wake mornings, wanting a man next to you. She splashes cold water against her face. She won't be nailed to her mother's bed. The night she spent with Chris she woke the next morning, her head on his shoulder, not certain where she was, who this man was. His arms held her and she felt his breath against the back of her neck. He could not be here but he was. That certain someone we can never summon or sum up. A ghost chasing a ghost. The circuitous path her life had taken turned back on itself.

III

I was only a girl. I had no idea what life would be. One day I sat with Petya along Nevsky Prospekt and watched women go by and we asked ourselves which one we would be. A young, wide-eyed woman with thick eyebrows, a full nose, and ivory skin wheeled a stroller by. She must be the wife of a civil servant. Look at her boots. They're saving for an apartment.

That one? The one who has stopped and leans against the bench. Look at how she follows a boat down the Neva. She had soulful eyes, fine, delicate lashes, an Aryan nose. She wore a blue business suit, the skirt just above her knees. Why had she stopped? It was a sunny day, a clear, blue sky overhead, the breath of breeze. A gull flew over our heads and dove towards the water. She turned and headed down the street. Where, we could not guess, but we knew that one day we would walk down that street as she did. We could not rush our future fast enough.

Petya tugged at my sleeve and nodded towards a woman in a tight-fitting white dress, bare at the shoulders, a black velvet ribbon tied around her neck. She had straight black hair down to her shoulders. Her lipstick was smudged and there were dark circles under her eyes. Was she an actress? A rich man's mistress? We rubbed shoes against cobblestones.

Do you remember the woman we saw yesterday? Petya asked. The one in a floor-length black velvet dress, her arms crossed across her breast, her eyes shut? You remember how she seemed to stagger. A man in a beret and black overcoat stood behind her. He had a moustache, rimless glasses, and looked as if he would go up to her. He reached out to her with a hand and then let it fall. In a moment she walked away. He looked at her until she disappeared.

Are you lost? Sergei asked the first time he saw Tania near the Hermitage. You seemed to hesitate. Your lips moved, as if you were talking to yourself. I get lost too. My mother worries that one day I'll disappear down some street and she'll never see me again. His pale blue eyes were amused. One day. He gestured down the street. When children are no longer children they leave home. His eyes sought out hers. She rubbed a hand against her dress. As if the blue had been washed out of his eyes. We'll never be able to find ourselves unless we get lost first.

Ten years later her uncle handed her a letter. Sergei was in Paris with his wife and child. How are you Tania? he asked. You did not want me to see you off at the train station, but I went anyway. I saw you stand in the middle of the station, your suitcase at your feet. This girl I thought whose cheekbones I touched, whose soft lips I kissed. You were my first love. My wife is a good woman, and I love her, but it's not the same thing.

For a moment Tania looked up. Outside, she heard the angry, exasperated voices of a couple in argument. She remembered a hand brush her cheek. My wife is a woman I could marry, she read. We could not. It was the first time she had seen his handwriting, but she knew it would be careful, precise. She got up and put on a tea kettle. So much time had passed.

At the train station in Leningrad, she remembers seeing a woman sit up straight, her ticket clutched in her hands on her lap. She wore a pale blue dress buttoned to the neck, a navy blue collar, puffed sleeves. Her eyes were blank. There was a man who sat hunched over nearby, his arms crossed on his thighs, a cigarette in one hand. He's done all he can, she thought. He can do no more. A man in a fur cap and gray overcoat with a scarf around his neck looked at Tania. The men who she knew even when she was thirteen would look at her that way.

She listens for the sounds of the night, the busy hum of traffic on a summer evening. Tonight she had not heard the couple next door argue. She hears the whistling of the tea kettle. How long it had been whistling she does not know. She should sweep the apartment. It had been so long since she had, but she did not feel like it. If she went out to *A Second Cup* or a bar. Her legs ache and she rests in the armchair for a moment while the tea steeps.

Her parents never said anything to one another. Her father gestured indifferently with his hand if he wanted more meat or potatoes. Her mother focused on her hands. Tania finished dinner as soon as she could so she could leave, but she could not go until she had eaten everything on the plate. After he drank his *chai*, father would say, I'm going out and wipe his mouth with a napkin. He would not return until the morning papers were out.

***

Chris lifts a hand in front of his face. Dark, thick veins, the skin creased, a pale white scar on his ring finger. He turns his hand over and examines the lines that crisscross and intersect on his palm. His fingers are furrowed, wrinkled like raisins.

Everyone knew but you, Alicia said. You had gone out with Diane. She takes a drag of her cigarette. What was it two months? I asked you whether you had met her friends yet. You said no and I told you she did not want you if she did not want you to meet them. For a moment Alicia paused, looked over his shoulder. We hoped it would work. We knew how much you wanted it.

His lower back ached. Last night he tossed and turned and had not been able to sleep. He had wakened with a stiff back and the drive to Montreal had been two- and-a-half hours.

For a moment he looks around a room he knows so well he no longer sees it. A standard hotel room for the middle class. Queen-sized bed. Desk. Coffee pot, cups, glasses, ice bucket. Imitation Impressionist landscapes on the wall.

It may not be cheap at home. It's never cheap on the road. You think you'll give yourself a break. You never do. Home may be where the heart is, but on the road home is the place you left.

I love you, Diane said before she kissed him the last time and got out of the car. She brushed strands of blonde hair off her forehead, her pale blue eyes large in her head, a sadness in them he could not redeem. He runs a hand over his bald head. Outside, a police siren loud before it faded. Gunfire, explosions from the television in the next room.

It's none of my business, Dan said. You've worked here.... What? Close to thirty years. You've done a good job. You have respect. All of a sudden you quit. Just like that. It doesn't make sense. He brushed unruly hair back from his forehead.

It's always greener on the other side of the street. We change our lives because we think that if we do everything will be better. For a moment he looked at Chris. We don't change. We are who we are. He sipped coffee. In a couple of months you'll want your job back. He examined the cup. It doesn't make sense. It never does.

Chris pours bourbon in his glass. He must have thought of Diane when he entered Tania. There was always someone else in bed with the woman he lay alongside. It might be his wife, his high school girl friend, a woman he met at a conference in Portland, even his mother. When he was ten, he dreamed he made love to an aunt. He would go to her home after school. She would give him Coca-Cola, play monopoly with him. Her breasts were firm and she laughed whenever he said anything.

He sees his hands unbutton Tania's skirt, slip it down,

pull her jersey up, take it off. He steps back to look at her. A hint of a smile on her face. Green eyes flecked with hazel luminous. The thick hair of her groin dark against her pale, gleaming body. With a finger she traces cardinal-red lips..

This afternoon, he went by a thin, sallow-skinned kid with a scraggly beard who had his hand out for money. His eyes were sunken in his head and there were dark circles under them. His dirty blond hair was unruly, long. Fuck, Chris thought. His shoes are more expensive than mine.

You middle class pig, the kid threw at Chris and trailed after him. You live off us. Wipe your ass with the work you force us to do. He passed Chris and blocked his path. You can't get it up for your women anymore and have to go to our women you've made whores. You think they want you? His voice rising. Chris went into a restaurant, ordered coffee, and waited. In a few minutes, the kid found someone else to harangue.

You don't understand why we are so tight with money his father said. You did not have to live through the Depression. We held on to what we had. He smiled and rubbed his bald head. We ate lard sandwiches. Chris had lived long enough now that he had as much a past as his father had. Too much of it had come out of the monthly paycheck. Insurance, retirement. An apartment, car. He had paid his dues, but wherever he looked there were more dues to pay. At one point he thought he knew what was due him but no longer did. He stayed at his desk and counted up the cost. An ulcer, headaches, tight back, chest.

Near Clark on Sherbrooke on his way back to the hotel, a man stepped forward from a doorway. A sickly-sweet smell of shit and alcohol came off him. There was a gap in his teeth and at the edge of his gums ulcers. His hand clamped Chris's arm. His voice hoarse, barely audible. Can you spare some change, sir?

Down the street there had been an insistent banging on a door and abruptly the shrill, piercing sound of a police siren. The man could not go on with it. He had been turned down too many times. His gaze fixed on something to the side of Chris. His exhaustion had taken him over. Only his hand would not let go.

Several months before he resigned his job his car hit ice on a sharp, downhill curve and all of a sudden slid sickeningly to the right. Chris turned the wheel sharply but the car began to slip sideways down the hill. He pulled the wheel hard right, the farmhouse to his left rushing up and then disappearing behind him, the car rushing towards a barb wire fence and woods, cutting through barbwire, crashing into bushes, stopping suddenly, abruptly, several feet from a maple. A thread of smoke rose from the engine.

He heard a rhythmic tap-tapping and at first did not know what it was. Then he saw his hand pounding the steering wheel. Outside, a loud, shrill *jay-jay* was repeated over and over, answered. Momentarily sun broke through an overcast sky and glanced off the side view mirror. Cautiously he stretched his legs.

He sees his hands crush the glass, shards of glass cutting sharply into skin, bourbon stinging raw tissue, ice cubes skidding across the end table, blood and bourbon spreading.

***

A *Second Cup* near McGill. Students have come and gone on their way to class or the library. Some read or worked on laptops. Those going to offices and stores take coffees to go. One or two men in suits work on laptops. A middle-aged woman in levis and turtleneck sweater writes in a notebook. One student looks out the window.

A grizzly, white-bearded man in a bulky coat and rubber boots comes in and approaches the men in suits but they ignore him. His coat and shiny, baggy pants look as if they had been thrown on a coat rack.. For a moment the heavy-set, old man looks around to see who else is in the *Second Cup* before he turns abruptly and leaves. Across the street, he approaches a woman at a bus stop.

Tania has read *The Gazette, Devoir, Voir, World,* which customers have left in the rack the *Second Cup* provides. She looked at a man in a pale blue tie and leather jacket come in. She watched him stop to light a cigarette after he stepped outside. The tie did not go with a leather jacket. The shirt was not the right color for the tie. She examined her nails, crossed her legs.

She did not like to lie about what work she had done, what education she had, what her skills were, but she had no choice. She had to ignore the impassive, intrusive scrutiny of her breasts and legs while they waited for her to answer. Young women were preferable, and although she was not old, she was no longer young. They did not care that older women knew the score, that they knew better than to demand or complain.

The people may change, but the story does not. She can describe the *Second Cup* in the morning with her eyes shut. *The problem is not that things change,* she writes in her notebook. *Just that they remain the same.* I know it's hard to live in Russia today, her mother wrote. I know why young people leave. But I'll never understand how anyone can leave home. I would be lost anywhere else.

You write, someone said. I see you always have a notebook. For a moment Tania looks up, thinking he is speaking to her, but she sees him talking to a woman in her forties at a table nearby. I know Sergei hurt you. In time, you'll get over him. His family was aristocratic, but they flourished, as if communism had never happened. Hers had been peasants communism had given an opportunity, but they were still peasants.

A man in a dark blue pinstripe suit, white shirt and paisley tie rested *Le Devoir* against a bloated paunch while he read. The woman in levis and black turtleneck sweater stopped to read what she had written. The two kids working behind the counter leaned against the counter and quietly talked. A man in a trench coat with graying hair, a full moustache, and a beet-red face glanced at Tania for a moment before he left.

Night after night her mother waited for her father to come home. She knew he had been with a woman, but pulled the covers back for him once he got home. At least the men who come to her bed fuck her. She runs a finger around the rim of the latte cup and stretches her legs. Her father returned to mother's bed every night no matter how late it was. Her men always found the door.

Love is loss, she tells Jeanne. No one walks hand-in-hand into the sunset anymore. You've not the met the right man, Tania. You fall in love before you know the man. I'm always someone else's dream, Tania answers.

Tania never spoke to Sergei. She was too young. She would not have known what to say. Go back to your fiancee, she told Robert. Next time you want to get fucked, go to a whore. It is what it is, she told Chris. Don't make something more of it. Antoine? What would she say to Antoine?

Why did you leave? Sergei writes. I would have found a way. You women! Robert replies. You want to get laid as much as men do, but you say it's love. Men think with their dicks you say. Don't think your cunt doesn't speak for you. Close your eyes, Chris says. I want you to feel my lips with your body. She sees Antoine approach. He never leaves.

Someone: pain.

Someone: cry.

Someone: silence
Someone: gone.

***

Renee, the bartender, comes from the Eastern Townships. You want another bourbon? she asks Chris. Herve, who was reading Hannah Arendt's *Eichmann in Jerusalem* when Chris sat down next to him told him he is here Friday and Saturday nights. He is French, from Brittany, works as a software programmer and was in Bangkok last year. He waves a hand in front of him. This year it is Montreal. Where he will be next year he does not know. This is a new wine, Renee says, pouring wine into Herve's glass. South African. Herve is short, with curly black hair, a thick moustache, a weak chin. His face is red and gleams with perspiration.

George is an engineer who worked on the Prince Edward Island bridge. He comes from a small town in Ottawa, but won't go back. He is a big man, with a burnt, chiseled face like granite, rust-brown hair that spills onto his forehead, thick, calloused hands. My mother's mother lived down the street, he says. You never escaped. He drinks beer. My grade school teacher not only taught the parents of her students but their parents as well. I knew how he would turn out she said about a drunk in town, a man who had left his wife, one whose business failed.

Chris tells them he is from Vermont. You need to get to Montreal, George grins. I know what small towns are like. Seven or eight times a year, Chris says. I came across the Cafe Saravejo a couple of years ago, Chris adds. They have a gypsy band. For a moment he runs a hand across his balding head. He laughs.

I had to leave, Renee says. I saw what my mother's life was like. She puts her elbows on the bar and leans forward.

She wears a black silk shirt open to the waist, the line of her breasts visible. She has dark red hair tied in a ponytail, her skin pale. I was not going to spend my life in a small town. Wryly she smiles. I sang in a church choir when I first got to Montreal. For a moment she looks around the bar to see if there is anything she needs to do and goes to the other side of the bar, begins to put glasses in water, others on shelves.

Why Hannah Arendt? Chris asks Herve. He shrugs his shoulders. In Bangkok, I was stuck in traffic for three hours every day on my way to work. The pollution was awful. Mercedes and BMWs — two hundred thousand dollars each in Bangkok — edged through streets crowded with out of work farmers from the north, girls who had been sent to Bangkok to be prostitutes.

He takes a sip of wine. I asked an Australian I worked with how he did it. Herve turns to me. It was madness, he adds. You need to be a Buddhist he said and if you can't be. He went to the Vietnam beaches weekends. Herve runs a finger across his moustache. He was gone before summer was out. I started reading. When you work in a foreign country, you have time on your hands. This is good, he tells Renee. For a moment he runs a finger around the lip of his wine glass. It got me reading, he says, looking away.

At least you stay in one place for a year, George says. I may be in Vancouver for a month, move over to Calgary, fly to Labrador while I'm still working in Calgary. He finishes his beer and gestures to Renee for another. The hotel I'm in looks like the one I was in yesterday. I can tell you where the bed will be, what the bedspread looks like, but some days I have to ask myself what city I'm in or what day of the week it is. On a project I may work weekends and evenings. He wipes his forehead with a handkerchief. I should be packed and shipped. For a moment he looks at something on the other side of the bar. Some days I feel I have.

I want to travel, Renee says. A guy took me to Plattsburgh one day. I might as well have been in the Eastern Townships. She sees a waitress come to the bar and goes over to fill drink orders. When she returns, she fills Herve's glass and raises her eyebrows in a question to Chris. Another bourbon? It's difficult for a single woman to travel. A friend of mine lived in Madrid for awhile. The first time she took the subway so many men grabbed her she felt she was lifted off the ground. Take a long hat pin, a friend said. When someone cops a feel, poke it at them. You can say you were adjusting your hat.

I'm not tall, but in Bangkok I was a giant, Herve says. The Thai are tiny. They seem so young. Even the old. I thought they were fragile, but they can work more than any white man. He takes a sip of wine. Sometimes I took walks and heard *farang, farang* follow me. Their word for foreigner. For a moment he looks at a tall, lithe blonde with a low-cut tank top who has taken a seat across from them at the bar. I've worked with people from all over the world. Germans. Norwegians. South Africans. Wryly he smiles. Work moves everyone along. Thai smuggle themselves to Australia for work.

One New Year's Eve, I took a plane from Labrador to Montreal, George says. The miners on the flight had not seen a woman for more than six months. It was unbelievable. I don't know how the stewardesses survived. The hookers were waiting at the gate in Montreal. It was the easiest money they ever made.

Most guys come here, look at their drink, look around to see who's here, Renee says. If they talk about anything, it's hockey. Every now and then a couple of guys talk about the market, but this is not the kind of place stockbrokers come to. She runs a rag across the counter. Of course, there's the guy who comes in and tells me that his woman has left him, but he knows she still loves him. I want to say, buddy, if she loves you what are you doing here getting drunk? She brushes hair back from her forehead.

We're not from Montreal, George says. We don't know anyone. We go to a bar, watch *Les Canadiennes* on the tv. Say something to the guy next to us. We go back to the hotel and watch more television, finish a beer. The evening is still young. We go out again. This time we may look for a woman. He runs a hand through his hair. Everyone in a bar is passing through. Tomorrow we won't be here. He nods to Herve. I know you're here every week, but you won't be here next year. Someone else will be in your place. Renee will be talking to him. If she's still here.

What do you think? Chris says to George, gesturing in the direction of the woman with the tank top across the bar. It's close to midnight on a Saturday night. She's been here a half hour. If she's meeting someone, it looks like he's not coming. Chris, you've lived in Vermont too long. She's a hooker. In a few minutes she gets up and goes to the washrooms. When she comes out she is wearing a micromini and boots and leaves the bar.

***

Tania edged to the curb when she passed a beggar on St. Catherine. Sometimes she crossed the street. They had been beaten to their knees and their eyes saw nothing, although early in the morning she saw how their glance followed the lone pedestrian like a dog its master.

I can't do more, Tania, Jeanne said. I just got this job myself. When the supervisor wants me to work overtime, I do it. When he puts his hand on my shoulder, I don't say anything. I don't know what I'll do if he does more. I need the job.

Businessmen go by, gesturing, saying what needs to be

said, closing deals, counting what needs to be counted. Girls in low-cut tank-tops and miniskirts or tight jeans and blouses open at the neck, laugh and talk excitedly on their way to shop. West of *Chapters* she began to see Arabs and Indians. Old women pushed carts. In Westmount, police moved them out of the neighborhood.

She would not waitress. She had once. At first, they did not understand her French. Then she had to be fluent in English. The way men looked at her at first made her feel desirable. But then. How men — even women —undressed her in a glance. If anything went wrong, she got it from all sides. Not only from customers but also the manager and cook. Even if nothing went wrong. Where had she gone? Didn't she understand? This is undercooked. Not what was ordered. Some nights she had gone into the service corridor to scream.

She had not seen her uncle in more than ten years, and was not certain how much Russian she still understood. She stayed with his family when she first came over from Russia, but it was clear he did it as a favor for her mother — his sister — and would do no more. Don't ever forget Russian, her mother wrote. You have to remember where you came from, but she was not where she came from and what family there was was not family.

I'd like to help, Charles, a friend of Jeanne's said yesterday, over lunch at the Greek restaurant on the corner of Parc. He gestured to the hostess for menus. Jeanne thought I might be able to do something, he added without looking at her. Charles had a pencil-thin moustache, hair slicked down with too much gel, a prominent Adam's apple. His seersucker suit had come from cheap outlet malls. He was young, callow and thought he knew something, but he was a boy, and Tania flustered him. If you ask me one more time how I'm doing? she thought. Why does he think I'm here? He had three quick glasses of wine and became a sloppy drunk. Tania did not say anything. Jeanne had made an effort.

A woman in a skin-tight dress and stiletto heels, her skin heavily rouged, lipstick coral red, leaned against a building on the corner of Montagne. It was barely noon. She did not seem to see anyone, but Tania saw how her eyes flickered and examined those who went by. She was perfection, blue eyes, blonde hair, almost silver, a body men would cry for. You would say she was waiting for someone.

While she waits for a light to change, Tania shuts her eyes. Her legs are heavy and her back stiff. Flickering electric flashes cross her mind. She sees a young couple hand-in-hand on St. Catherine, a teenage black in baggy pants and baseball cap turned backward, a gray-haired, middle-aged man in a suit carrying a briefcase walking with a tall blonde in sheath dress and heels. She sees herself leaning back against a store window in baggy khaki trousers, a stained, gray cloth coat, a torn scarf around her neck, styro foam cup in her hand. Her boots are split at the heel. If you can help, she says, her voice indistinct, almost a whisper. Her eyes filmed over, averted.

***

At twenty-five, fresh out of graduate school, the world his oyster. There was nothing that stood in his way. It did not matter what it was. So much for.

At thirty-five, he glimpsed something at the edge of his consciousness, as if, somehow, something flashed before it faded. He did not think about it. He was still young. There was so much he had to do, even if it was more of an effort than it had been.

At fifty-five hemmed in, buffeted at every turn by workshops, meetings, training. Everyone had to be on the same page. For far too long Chris had to play the game. He did what he no longer wanted to do. Long sleepless nights eyeballing the ceiling he would see a bare room with a single light bulb as if he had just stepped into it.

You refuse to be brought in, Diane said. You get along, follow the rules of the game, but everyone knows you don't buy into it. It bothers them. You stand aside and they don't know what to make of it. As if you're judging them.

You like comfort, but it makes you uncomfortable. Wryly she smiled. The working class stiffs I know have no problem forgetting where they came from. For a moment she took his hand. I don't know what it is. You resist the world.

His first weeks in Montreal Chris walked for hours. He would stop for an espresso or beer when he felt like it. Sometimes he thought he saw Tania and would follow the woman for a few blocks until he realized it was not her. Near the Museum of Fine Arts one day, he saw Ed and his wife from his town in Vermont. Ed stopped and looked at Chris, took a step forward, but when Chris looked through him Ed thought he must have been mistaken and went by.

One day in his room he sat in an armchair and contemplated a spider spinning its web on the sill of the window, a towel hanging from the bathroom door, a magazine clipping of Jimi Hendrix he had put in a dime-store frame.

Yesterday at the park near Mont Royal, he stopped to watch a stooped, white-haired man on crutches fling a frisbee for his dog to chase. His face was pock-marked, wrinkled, ravaged by alcohol. When the Irish Retriever returned with the frisbee, he laughed, patted the dog on its flank, playfully pulled at its fur. All of a sudden Chris's stomach contracted with a stabbing pain and for a moment he staggered. Sometimes when he stood he felt light-headed and would reach for a chair or table to steady himself.

Did you ever imagine you would do something else? Pete asked him one evening at the end of their shift at *The Gazette*.

A proofreader is not the job anyone wants. For a moment Chris looked at Pete. Pete's face was always flushed and he would often wipe his forehead with a handkerchief while he worked. His work amused Pete. Chris did not know what to say.

***

Do you remember the first time we met? Jeanne asked. We were in *The Gap* in the Eaton Centre looking for blouses. We both turned to the mirror at the same time to see how we looked and discovered we both had on the same blouse. She laughed. We went out to have wine. I'll never forget the look on that guy's face when you told him to shove it when he said something about your ass. The blouse was pale blue, with navy blue flowers stitched at the lapels. Do you remember?

Jeanne looks at Tania and when she does not respond, turns away and begins to stack dishes in the drainer. She has had to bail Tania out too many times. If it was not a man, it was a job or landlord. Something always kept it from working out. For a moment Jeanne holds a cup in her hands and looks out the window before she puts it in the drainer. It's none of her business. She turns away from the sink and wipes her hands with a dish towel. Her face caves in on itself. I'm tired, she says. I'm going to read in bed.

When Tania first arrived in Montreal, she answered an ad for models and Pierre, who was a friend of Jeanne's hired her. He taught painting at UQAM. She did not mind posing nude. The only time I see you relaxed is when you're naked, Antoine said. On the street or in a restaurant, you try to be someone you think you should be, but you're not sure you can pull it off. You hesitate, shred napkins, break off conversation, look away. Your back is rigid, tight. In bed, you're comfortable with your body. You don't care what anyone thinks.

You can balance your checkbook, Pierre said. Think about what you need to buy at the grocery. Once I put you in position you can't move. Don't worry about how they see you. You're a problem for them to solve. Your body can defeat them. It's not easy for them. Or for you. You want to shift position. It's tiring. We can't find many middle-aged models. She heard he had been on the wagon, but dark red veins still crisscrossed his nose. There were dark circles under his eyes. Kids love modeling. It's an easy way to make money. Help them through school. Earn spending money.

For a moment he looked around *La Presse* and rubbed his eyes. His chest sagged. By the time you're middle-aged. He drank coffee and grimaced, pressed a hand against his belly. You have a job, a career, family. Sometimes mothers apply when their children are old enough for school. Wryly he smiled. His eyes were tired. I know it's only stop-gap.

What I do is my business, Tania thinks, but I can't piss Jeanne off. She goes over to the tv and turns it on with the sound off. I can't be stupid. On the screen, a young man with ears that stuck out like Alfred E. Newman, frowned, bit his lip. When he gave the right answer, he wiped his brow, smiled, glanced at the audience, pleased.

She leans back against the couch and rubs her brow. The first week looking for work she was enthusiastic, excited. Last week, she was tired and did not show up for several interviews. She had no chance to get those jobs, but had talked herself into trying. It was We'll get in touch, we'll call back, if you were to take some night classes, work weekends, nights. She runs a finger along the arm of the couch. Even if you turned the sound up, it would make no difference.

Every evening on Jeanne's couch, Tania rolled over, rolled back. Brought her legs up, straightened them out. Stared at the ceiling, counted sheep. She needs a man, needs to take him in her mouth. Sometimes she wants to hold Jeanne, kiss her lips, run her tongue over her neck, open her blouse and push her bra up, take her pale, heavy breasts into my mouth, suck them as men suck mine. In a moment, she balls up a handkerchief and stuffs it into her mouth, bites down hard. Let them fuck her over. She did not care.

***

I prefer the evenings there is no band the Serb says. The music makes my head pound and my heart race. I remember nights back home. For a moment I forget I'm old. I can't take it.

He puts a hand on the shoulder of a Rubenesque, raven-haired woman sitting next to him. She is wearing a scoop-necked navy blue dress and her pale skin is freckled above her breasts. Denise came into the Cafe Saravejo one night, he says. I don't know why. For a moment he massages his forehead and looks down at his beer. His face is oily and glistening and there are folds of flesh under his chin.

Women who come into bars are looking for men he says. I knew she would not be looking for me. Tenderly he looks at her, his eyes clouded over. She sat next to me, and asked how I was. You know it doesn't mean anything. It's just talk. He runs a hand through sparse, scraggling hair. I don't know what it was. I don't know why. I told her. She listened. He signals the bartender for another beer.

Denise says something to Chris in French, but he does not understand and looks to the Serb. His French is not good enough. For a long moment Denises examines Chris and says something more to the Serb. Her deep black eyes large in her head. She likes the people here the Serb translates. They don't forget where they come from.

She had to get away from her family as soon as she could. She went to London, Paris, Amsterdam. She loved

Amsterdam. Denise looks at Chris to see if he has understood. For a moment she searches for something in her purse. She modeled for artists.

How'd she get to Montreal?

She was born here, but that's not why she came back. She leans towards the Serb, runs a hand across his bald scalp and kisses him on the cheek. I do know why, but that may not have been the reason. For a moment she runs several fingers across her forehead. The first time she came to the Cafe Saravejo she felt at home. For a moment the Serb places a hand against Denise's cheek. He runs a finger down her nose and laughs. She grabs his hand and holds it in her lap.

Il est un artiste, Denise says turning to me. She runs a hand through short, curly hair. Did he understand? her glance asked. *Un artiste.*

Not anymore the Serb says to Chris. He sips his beer and shrugs his shoulders. I wasn't any good. I stopped going to the studio. He looks at the bartender and signals for another beer. My wife left me.

Denise says something to the Serb and he nods. She knows that look on my face. The first time she met me she knew I had stopped living. What do you expect from life? she asked. You think the world owes you something? You're alive, aren't you? Attentively she listens to him and smiles, her cheeks dimple.

What does he do?

I work for *The Gazette*. It's a job. How did she like Europe?

Denise takes a cigarette from a pack in her purse and listens to the Serb translate while she lights it. Deeply she inhales and for a moment looks across the bar. Lipstick has smudged her lips and she dabs at them with a Kleenex.

She loved Europe. She did not have to know much of the language to model. She got by. When you're young. He waved his hand around the bar. Nothing gets in the way.

Why did she come home?

Her life has not been easy. She met her husband in Europe. He was a sculptor. They came back to Montreal, but he was hit by a truck. You can guess how it is. She loves him, but she deserves more from life. There's not much she can do.

For a moment she listens to what the Serb says and then grabs Chris's hand and holds it against her thigh. *L'amour,* she says. For a moment she runs a finger over the back of Chris's hand. *L'amour fou* the Serb says, a wry smile on his face.

The Serb pushes off from his bar stool and circles Denise, his hands exploring the space in front of him, carving air. He leans towards her, almost stumbling, and then moves away to the middle of the dance floor. Slowly he turns, as if he is a moon circling its planet. Round and round, moving away, returning, retreating, until his circles wind themselves tightly around themselves and he is close enough to her to put his face in hers. She smiles and pushes against his chest.

***

Tania, they say. That's how they begin. Tania. They look around to see who is in the club tonight. Lips curled down. Sure of themselves. You do the club scene?   You come here often?   Laughter behind her. *That I have to do this. That I.* Laughter I recognize as my own.

Thick, dark hair brushed across his forehead, glasses with thin steel frames, pale ivory skin. A black turtleneck sweater, black trousers shiny at the knees, black dress shoes

Lanky, thinning sandy hair brushed forward onto his forehead, sunken eyes. A suit, white shirt, dayglo blue tie.

Straight jet-black hair down to his shoulders, thin lips held tightly together, a hawk nose. A black shirt, open at the neck, khakis.

Sunken eyes. Washed-out eyes, blue, bloodshot. Chestnut

brown eyes, large in his head. Half-closed eyes, slits, blank. That examine, judge, undress.

After an hour or so, the club becomes stifling from so many bodies crowded together. Her underwear is damp with perspiration. She's not young. Small breasts. The only tank top she has threadbare. If it would only rain. A pain begins to throb in the middle of her forehead.

Washed out, blue, bloodshot stops.. I look at him. I look around the club. I look at my hand holding a wine glass. Long fingers with silver-blue nails. Wrinkles on the back of my hand I cannot smooth.

He checks off his list. He has it down pat. If I don't smile. If my eyes don't meet his. If I am nervous. He counts the possibilities. If I would, will, can be had. It makes no difference. I will be had.

Tania they ask. Do you want more wine? Pinot Grigio, right? A gold band on his ring finger. A large signet on his middle finger. Some of them take their rings off before they go to the club. The sour smell of sweat and alcohol. A patient smile. Yes. Pinot Grigio. I imagine his fingers against my cheek, the gold band on a ring finger glinting in morning light. It is Tania, right? After two or three drinks, the alcohol hit her stomach like a blow.

Half-closed, slits, blank at her side. A baseball in his throat for an Adam's apple. His forehead wet. He wipes it with a handkerchief. He's never been here before. His friends say he needs to get out, meet some women. They tell him he has a wry humor. He is kind, dependable. The right woman will straighten him out. He knows his friends are right. He should try.

Divorced long enough to prize his freedom. What he missed all those years of married bliss. He takes his glasses off and cleans them with a handkerchief. For a moment examines a fingernail. Excuse me, he says. I need a drink.

Chestnut-brown, large approaches. His smile a delight. Swarthy, with a sharp, hawk nose, full, strong jaw, shaved head. A black sweater and trousers from Armani or Prada. When she gets home and gets into bed, she will think of Armani, sleep a restless sleep.

Tania they say. That's a nice name. Tania. Last night it was Kelly.

You know how it is they say. Tania right?

I've seen you before they say. I know I have.

You know what's what they say.

The conversations they carry on in their head. The evenings they plan. The nights they dream.

A redhead with a rose tattooed on her shoulder. A blonde with tight levis on the dance floor. A woman with long black hair and micromini whose laughter rose above the hubbub. Everywhere she looks in the club she doesn't find herself.

Some evenings — most evenings — nothing happens and she find herself leaning against a wall at the end of the evening. Blue-gray cigarette smoke a haze in the club, the air heavy. The dance floor deserted, except for a few couples hanging on to one another. It's too late for a bus or subway. She never thinks to bring enough money for a taxi. In the morning she doesn't look at herself in the mirror.

Something about her or about men she doesn't understand. Love, they say. Abruptly she laughs. Sometimes they don't. Sometimes she doesn't care. The men who force themselves on her. Force her body to respond until she cries out. If they knock on the door she thinks. This time

IT WAS

The sky cloudless, pale blue, azure. There was no wind. Workmen were at work on a building across the quad. A few minutes before the end of the hour. In the distance a squirrel raised itself on its hind legs, as if it had heard something. The only sound that of Fran pushing a chair back.

The day paused, waiting to begin. A day yet to happen. A day already past.

It had been morning.

Elena looked at him to ask why he was here. Her eyes were tired. Her skin puffy, lipstick smeared. What is it? she asked.

There was nothing to say but what had to be said. Nothing to say he had not already said. He could no longer do this.

She brushed hair back from her forehead, pulled her robe together, her breasts briefly visible. She would make tea. At the far end of the couch there were stains of semen.

It had been night.

He called. I've not seen him in years. How can I not see him? In college I was in love with him.

Elena was eighteen when she met him, a freshman in college. He was her first love.

The cutting edge slices in and before you know what has happened you see the blood, feel it wet and hot, and only then does understanding come.

She would not die for love again, but he was back. What it would be this time he did not think that even she knew.

He read, drank scotch, went to bed, did not sleep, drank more scotch, got up to pee, pointed himself in the direction of the toilet. For a moment he staggered and with an effort held himself up, silent, suddenly afraid, his breathing collapsed on itself. He was sweating.

At the emergency room, they took blood, checked vital signs, probed, asked questions, shrugged their shoulders. It could be. It was not. It might be. He should not worry unless

For weeks afterward he did not sleep, eat. He avoided cafes Elana liked, looked at the phone but did not pick it up, drove by her home late at night. He drank. In need of...

The day continued.

Outside two students went by, followed by a group of four, then a lone student. On their way to another class, the student union, dorm. One student pointed to something he could not see. Another gestured. A jay perched on a branch of a tree. A squirrel motionless with a nut in its paws.

Fran looked up from the manuscript she examined. The calendar said there was a meeting at four with Martin who was teaching Melville this term. The in-box had nothing pressing. His hand motionless on the desk, as if it had its place alongside the stapler, pad, calendar and phone that lay across its surface.

The hospital....

Elena had asked for him. There'd been an accident. She had been crossing College Street and been hit by a car. Just before noon. She walked everywhere, but walked as if someone else, not her, did the walking, an eggshell walk which convinced men she did not know her body.

Elena did not ask. She was there when she wanted to be and not when she was not. It might be a concert, movie, dinner. Her husband, a friend, friends. A lover. A walk in the woods. It might be nothing. It did not matter.

I won't be tied down. Not by my husband. Not by you. Understand.

Insistent, eyes wide with anger. It was not his business. For Elena uncertainty was possibility, chance opportunity. It did not concern him.

One day she came to the library and asked him about

a book. He had seen her in town. She was attractive, with short, curly black hair, cobalt blue eyes, dimpled cheeks, a rosebud of a mouth, a distant smile on her face, delicately shaped breasts. Her laughter bubbled up at odd moments, husky and full.

The next time they said hello. They talked. They had coffee in cafes. They talked more. Then.

Some whispered words. An agreement to meet.

Then.

A quick embrace.

A wet kiss full of promise.

He remembers the first time they made love he had come out of the bathroom afterwards and not knowing what he would say said that this was not playing, he wanted them to risk something, that there was too much compromise in life, too much sacrifice of desire to comfort, and he was sick of it. She sat on a chair with one leg lifted, her foot on the seat, her chin resting on a knee, and looked at him in a way he did not understand.

A friend. An accident. I need to go. Call Martin. Tell him I can't see him today.

Polish blue eyes looking into his: here, now.

Night the First

He was the receptionist asked. Right. Elena was down the hall.

A doctor came up. He ran a hand across his forehead. There were dark circles under his eyes. Elana's tibia and femur were broken. She'd be in a thigh-high cast for months. For a moment he looked at something down the hall.

She'd been crossing College Street. For a moment he looked at him before he continued. The driver had seen her, but she did not seem to see him. He tried to turn but could not. He could do nothing he said. As if he'd been. He did not know how to say it. Drugged, hypnotized.

When they put her onto the stretcher she sat up suddenly the doctor said. As if she did not know what had happened until that moment.

She closed her eyes, whispered something. It was not a prayer. It might have been a name.

Elena was asleep. Her face puffy, red. Her mouth slightly open. She clutched the blanket.

The nights he looked at her after they made love, a slight smile on her face, the tip of her tongue pressed against an upper lip, breath a whisper. Sound of Hovaness on a late-night Albany FM station. Her skin luminous in moonlight.

At the hospital after his fourth heart attack, father looked up at him but did not know who he was. He looked at the nurse as if she would know. He closed his eyes. His skin was stretched tight across his forehead. Wisps of white hair across it. Breathing tubes in his nose. The skin of his lips cracked. White stubble of a beard on his face. You can't stay the nurse said. He's weak. He tires easily.

Father refused to see doctors and would not go to a hospital. He did not trust them. His children were born at home. Once he cut his foot with a razor while trimming a callus. It was not until the infection reached his groin — a pulsing red streak up his leg — that mother called the doctor.

The day he died mother had visited him at the nursing home where we had moved him from the intensive care ward of the hospital. He had kissed her, told her that he loved her, had always loved her. He wanted her to know that. On her way home she said she had to go back.

There's something. He.....

When she entered his room a nurse was feeding him chicken soup but he could not swallow any of it. He tried to say something to the woman he had spent more than 50 years with, but she could hear nothing. He would not let go of her hand and she had to forcibly remove it when the nurse put her hand on her shoulder and said he was gone.

You're here.

For a moment Elana wet her lips with her tongue. She reached for his hand. He was not sure who <u>you</u> was. Her husband. Her first love. There were others.

That he was here....

The him he was. The one who could not be other than who he was.

Do you remember....

She trailed off, looked away from him. There were moments she'd say something, look away for a moment, not finish what it was. Her eyes would become distant. She no longer heard what was said. She'd been somewhere else, she'd say when she came back.

She'd pick up a cup and be surprised a few minutes later that she held it in her hand. Hello she would say, touch his cheek. It was nothing. In a moment she would laugh. It was something but not anything she could tell him.

You were not there.

There was always someone else. The day that Mansfield came into the café. She had not seen her in weeks. The night Elena invited him to her home for dinner. He should meet her husband, friends. Before they spent a weekend in Montreal, she had to see Ann. She had to say something to her. Something she must know.

Someone she knows. Someone she must meet. Someone she does not know but who she is sure she'll meet. That if she does not meet

For a moment she looked at him, before her glance trailed down to her leg. Distractedly she touched the cast.

There is no one.

When her first love left her, she did not want to live but did not die. When he came back years after she had last seen him, it was no longer him. Can he get her the glass of water?

She is never alone. There are dinners, concerts, movies, cafes, parties. Someone is always there. Someone shows up. Someone does not go away. We they say. The night that. The day they. The he dids. The she saids.

She cannot escape. They ask, arrive. She smiles, laughs, nods yes. They ask her to go with them. She does. She cannot help herself.

She can. She does not answer the phone. She walks in woods by herself. She leaves town weekends and it is no one's business where she has gone.

She wants nothing more than to draw, read a book, look out the window, walk by herself in woods, imagine what might happen, and if not that, something else. What it might be.

Then.

Perhaps.

She waits for then.

It was….

She remembers a day, one day, wet, warm, full of mists.

Warblers and sparrows darted back and forth in front of them as they walked a trail to the water's edge. Somewhere in the woods a woodpecker worked away at a tree. His hip was soft, yielding, when it touched hers. Later they lay on grass in a gently sloping field talking of childhood. She ran her fingers down his thigh. He traced with his the shape of her lips.

Of course....

They will come to visit her at the hospital but not know what to say. How are you? they will ask. Can we get you anything? Do something? Arrange your pillow? Ask the nurse for? The saying they must.

They will ask about the accident. It was she will begin, but stop, look away. She cannot finish. It cannot be told. She will make an effort, but as much as she wants to tell it she knows she cannot. In any case it is hers. Hers alone.

This afternoon....

She read a magazine that had been given her but could not concentrate on what she read. She talked to nurses, but they left to see other patients. She slept.

After she woke, she did not feel like reading. She could watch tv but does not watch tv, as he knows. She stopped her husband from buying one. After awhile she noticed the ceiling. Of course she would. She was flat on her back.

She does not remember how long it kept her attention. At some point. She does not know how to say this. At some point the ceiling knew who she was. As if it had seen it all before. As if it could tell her.

She shook her head, bit her lip. For a moment she ran a hand across her forehead. As if talking about it disturbed her.

Its story. Its story, she repeated, as if she had already told him what it was.

She tires of talk. No one says anything except what she has heard before. It bores her. Sometimes she bores herself when she hears herself. She turned away.

It was not until she stared at the ceiling that
She heard it speak. She was sure she did.

He must listen. If he cannot. For a moment she glanced at her hand holding kleenex. Every room has a ceiling. We don't know it's there but it is. She balled the tissue up and dropped it on the bed. As we are not.

It can be.....

As if she has stopped him on the street, taken his arm. Knocked on his door, announced herself. Called at three in the morning, said

Whatever says has to say.

Her hand over her face, its own agent.

We wake she said. The day is. She touches the cast. Not what we want it to be. We turn over. If w could only sleep a few minutes longer. The dream did not end but we don't remember what it was. We make tea.

The day waits. We go for a walk. We see a friend. He says. She asks. We answer. We go to a café. No one is there except someone we don't want to see. We stop at a store to get something for dinner. We go down the street but see no one nor anything that interests us.

We go home. The cat sleeps on the couch. Flowers on the kitchen table have wilted. We must make dinner but don't feel like it. We look in the fridge. Have a second glass of wine. After dinner we read but put the book down. For a moment we close our eyes.

Day after day the ceiling says. Day after day the same. Day after day failure.

Does he think that he. That she. They....

She wets her lips with her tongue, runs a finger across them.

Touch me.

Night the Second

She'd been asleep. Suddenly she saw Isabelle Adjani, Adele H., Victor Hugo's daughter, in the Truffaut film, approach the officer she loves but who does not love her.

Adele, he says, but she does not hear him. She walks by him, eyes blank, face blasted, a woman scorned, lost, her love refused, life gone. For a moment Elana turned away. Her hand traced lines on the blanket.

It was not….

She grimaced. She was not sure that he would understand what she would say. She was not sure herself. Would he get her a glass of water? After she drank she held the glass in her hands and for a moment examined it That a woman would cross an ocean to be with the man she loves Adele H. had written in her journal. That a woman would do this.

It was….

Something she did not remember or had not noticed. That had not been there before. She put the glass down. It was not important. In any event.

He must have seen the film. She was not certain why she'd seen it but everyone had. Everyone said she should. She'd gone to see it but had been distracted, thinking about what she might do afterward, whether they would go to the café or the new bar in town. Ann had heard good things about it. She had just read *Lolita* and wanted to talk about it. She….

She had been with the Hamiltons. Ann mentioned the film this afternoon. She does not know why. They had not been talking about films. Ann had said something about Jeanne, a friend of theirs. What had happened to her.

He thought of Adele H., having opposed her father to cross the ocean to America to be with the man she loves. She sends him love notes he does not answer. She follows him wherever he goes. One day she sneaks into his room at the fort in Halifax to confront him.

The nights he drove by Elana's house to see if there was a strange car in the driveway, the house dark.

What could not be silenced sat alongside him the months he had not seen Elana demanding it be named, as real now as it had been at the beginning.

She did not know what to make of it. She'd seen the film before in college and liked it. She may have seen herself as Adele H. then, but she was young and did not know anything then. Why she had the dream. She gestured with a hand to take in.

Whatever.

Women....

They can never be just friends with a man. That does not mean they'll sleep with anyone. There must be. For a moment she smiled as if she remembered something. There must be

They talked close to a year before they kissed. She smiled. Before they understood what their talk said. She put her hand on his. Before it could be answered.

She cannot fuck anyone. She laughed. At moments though she cannot resist when the moment presents itself. She ran one finger across the top of his hand. She knows it has been difficult for him. In a low voice, as if she were talking to his hand.

If there is one man for Elana, there must be another. There must be at least two. If one leaves, there is always one left. She would never be left alone again, as she had been in college.

There was her husband, and if he were no longer her husband, there would be another husband. There would always be a husband.

You can't let....

For a moment she noticed a nurse pushing a patient in

a wheelchair down the corridor. She glanced at her cast, touched it.

Elena did not know how she made it back after she slit her wrists in college. She did not tell her father. Did not tell anyone. Months went by she does not remember. One day she slept with three men in six hours.

She met her husband. No. She did not meet him. One day he was there. One day she

It's a story he does not have to know.

He….

She knew that he should be the first one to come to the hospital. Some of the others. She waved a hand around the room. They. She closed her eyes.

The first time they met she asked him about a book. He asked her why she was interested. It was. He smiled. It was not.

He spoke of Dostoyevsky. She of Tolstoy. There was Flaubert. Not to mention Virginia Woolf. If she were to look at. Not if he had not read.

At one point she looked at him. She was sorry. She did not know where the time had gone. She had to go. She had to meet someone. It was all right he said. He had to. There was a lecture he had to be at. She smiled. He shrugged.

Did he remember….

She'd come to his apartment.

It had not been the first time. They talked, drank wine. He touched her hand to make a point. She ran a finger across a lip before she said. She looked at the clock. It was late. She rolled her eyes. He laughed. The bottle was empty. He opened another.

She does not remember who first leaned across the couch. They kissed. It seemed no more than a moment, but it took in the night..

She remembered the moment she touched him. He was hard. So hard. She had been wet. So wet.

She was wet now. She took his hand and slipped it under the sheets to show him. Cobalt blue almond-shaped eyes, flecked with gold, misting. It had come upon them so suddenly.

He never thought anything would happen. He may have inadvertently brushed her breast or touched her hand to emphasize something he said. He thought of what it would be like, but that did not mean

They talked. All they had done was talk.

You....

She held his hand, shut her eyes. Her face strained, lips pressed tightly together. He may not be the one who should be here, but his presence brought him forth. She squeezed his hand, coughed. Her brow furrowed, wet with perspiration. She slept. He does not remember how long.

He could not keep his eyes open. He too must have slept. At one point he saw himself running through a field. The sky overhead cloudless, azure blue. A slight cool wind brushed his face. An end of summer September day. The field had been freshly cut by a farmer for hay. He ran with the grace of an animal. His pace sure, easy. He felt he could run forever. His head fell forward and jerked him upright.

He remembered a nurse taking Elana's pulse, checking the IV, giving her pills. He rubbed his eyes, glanced at Elana. Her breath in and out, slow, even. A murmur.

He remembered the day she held his hand and told him that the line crossing the center of his hand meant that he would find love, that this line, here — she pointed to it — meant that he was dependable. He could be trusted. That this line. She looked away. She would not speak of it.

For a moment Elana opened her eyes, looked at him but did not see him. Suddenly she grabbed the sheet and pointed to something she saw over his shoulder but what it was he did not know. He was not sure that even she knew.

Night the Third

A nurse finished taking Elana's blood pressure, recorded the results on the chart at the base of the bed, glanced at the chart. She looked up, nodded to him. She would not say anything but would not have to say anything. It was a small town.

Elana was asleep. Her face drawn, pale. There was spittle on her lips. In one hand she clutched kleenex. Her breath labored.

She had called him this afternoon, said she did not want to see anyone, but he had to come. She needed to have him there. She would not be much company. He should know that. If she had to talk to anyone, be pleasant. Today had been

She did not finish.

He was patient. Unlike most men who blew up at the slightest moment, threw things, stormed out of rooms. She did not know what to make of him. Perhaps that was why

She did not finish.

She knew exactly who he was. He was the man who said no but would not say no to her.

Last night her husband had been at the hospital. Why he was not there tonight he did not know. At one point he'd been in Boston a month and rented an apartment. He has to be there Elana said. If he is not.

He had gone to the neighborhood bar. He knew everyone there. Some of them were married but he had never seen them with their spouses, although he had seen some of their wives out together. A night out by themselves was needed to maintain the balance of their marriages. For some it seemed many nights out. There were those who would never marry and the bar was as close to a home as they had.

He had been married. He had been in love, but at some point he realized he no longer knew what love was. Whether what they had — whatever it was — was enough to keep them together. They liked the same books, films. They gardened together. Their families were both working class. It was not as if one of them had married up.

It did not seem enough.

They no longer knew what they wanted. They could not talk about it because they feared what would come out. They did talk about it but what seemed obvious was no longer obvious.

At some point they knew it was over. The stranger who lay alongside them in bed had not been a stranger before. He does not remember whether he said something or she had but once it had been said it was a relief.

Elana wanted to know what his wife was like. When they fell in love. Why they married. What had happened. Why he had not re-married.

He had been in love. Then he was not.

That's how men were. They do not want to know.

You go round and round on the merry-go-round. You see men, women and children go by. At some point you realize that you always come back to the same place. You know that if you do this the rest of your life, you have no life. You stop, get off, look around to see who is there. The one that you will marry will appear.

If a woman was not married by a certain age. You did not want to be that woman. She'd seen her too many times. She lets every man take her, but no man keeps her, even if they do for a night, a week, months. Everyone knows her and turns away.

She….

She would not be her.

If a woman was married. For a moment she looked out

the window as if something she saw caught her attention. Marriage trapped so many women, but it would not trap her.

She lay back, put a handkerchief to her mouth. Her forehead was wet, strands of hair pasted against it. There were dark circles under her eyes. A bruise on her cheek. A raw red scar just below her chin.

Nights he was at her home she spent minutes washing her face, putting lipstick on, arranging her hair, selecting a nightgown before she came to bed.

The first night at the hospital she had prepared herself for visitors, brushed her hair, put lipstick on, applied a touch of rouge to her cheeks as she did at home. This was not like anything she had experienced before. Nurses and doctors around her, police. Friends coming to visit. Everyone wanted to hear what happened. What it was like.

Tonight she did not want anyone to see her. The nurse said she had a fever. This afternoon she vomited after lunch.

In college one summer she had gone to Yugoslavia. A dark, strange, mysterious land so unlike America. The home of Dracula, the witch Baba Yaga, mysteries unheard of.

She had a hunger in the soul. A life to be lived.

She was alone. She would not be alone long.

In Belgrade she met a man. He said she looked like a Roma. She did not understand what he meant. A gypsy he explained. They live by their own rules and have no place they can call their own. Whatever you have he said. He waved a hand to the left and then to the right. Is theirs. She should hear some gypsy music. There was nothing like it. If she were interested.

The music had been guttural, harsh. Like no music she had heard before. As if it had no beginning nor end. As if she heard it less than she heard herself. She would always hear it. Like no music she would ever hear again. A voice, sound.

Everyone was dancing. On tables. On the bar. A man

circled her. Another man. A woman. Everyone pressing up against one another.

She felt like shit the next morning. The man was no longer lying beside her. She did not know where she was. She got up, found a door. A silver-haired crone in some long shapeless black dress looked at her from the corner of a room before she continued sweeping with a broom.

In another room three bodies lay sprawled on a mattress. In a kitchen a man sat at a table with his coffee and did not notice her. When she stood in front of him long enough, he pointed — door, street.

Down the street a man played a violin in front of a bear. A woman lifted her skirts and circled the bear. A crowd had gathered. Elana buttoned her blouse, tucked it in, stood at the edge of the crowd. The woman went up to the bear, touched its cheek.

She remembered a church, a tavern. The man. What did he say his name was? Boris, Evgeny? He had led her past a church, turned at a tavern. The woman took the bear's paws, urged him to dance. The bear roared. The violin sawed back and forth.

She did not know where she was. Somehow. She does not know how. She found the train station.

In some village on the way from Zagreb to Belgrade she got sick. The meat must have been bad. The water not good. She clutched her abdomen, bit her lip. She shit. She shit and shit and could not stop.

She did not know how long she lay on some pallet in some house. It might have been a hospital. Women cleaned her. Every now and then someone came in and looked at her. A man examined her, gave her some pills.

Only her father knew she was in Yugoslavia, but he did not know where. He would not know how to find her. The American embassy was in Belgrade. She did not know where she was.

She does not know how long she lay there. It must have been days. She did not remember anyone or anything. One day her father was at the door. She did not know who it was.

In the neighborhood he grew up in he remembered the *pepper-regs* man come down the street with his cart calling out for paper, rags. Everyday an elf of a man, a Russian immigrant, walked a wolfhound down the street. A pig was roasted on the Dubinsky lawn Saturdays. Live chickens were slaughtered in basements.

The neighborhood was called duck town, because all the streets were named after birds — robin, lark, quail. None of the churches had services in English. Duck town was duck town not because its streets were named after birds but because it was foreign, strange. Ducktown did not belong.

His childhood was no less real than Elana's had been in Bronxville but when she spoke of what she had done or where she had been he was convinced that she was drawn to people and places that Bronxville rejected in order to throw them back in its face as he had not.

For a moment she grimaced. A cry escaped her. She was given morphine, but did not take it because she wanted to take it at home later. She took a tissue from the stand at the side of the bed and spit something into it. She lay back, her mouth open, saliva on her lips. She did not see him. She did not know he was there.

The first time they met she said he undressed her with a look. She smiled. A smile he did not understand. A faint fleeting smile. The silence of a moment that could not speak but did. The woman who would make him hers stood in front of him.

He remembered a day they had gone to a nature trail outside town. They walked, picked flowers, saw birds, chipmunks, once a rabbit, got tired, lay down. He braided her hair with wild flowers, traced her lips, unbuttoned her blouse. She held his head in her hands before she kissed him.

Elana lay with her back towards him. She needed to have him there and he was. She could sleep. When she woke she knew he would be there.

Once she left the hospital she would stay with her husband, see lovers. She could not be other than she was. She would see him if he did so on her terms. If he did not....

A man he no longer cared for but could not escape. He leaned back in his chair, stretched his legs, glanced at Elana. He rubbed his eyes. He had to sit the night through with him.

It's like this.

One hand washes the other. One hand puts itself against a cheek. One hand turns the pages of a manuscript. Eyes see out a window first thing in the morning. Eyes see a door open. Eyes see what they had not seen before. Ears hear an alarm clock, sirens, someone cough.

One did not call when he should. The second made sure the door was locked. The third took the pot off the stove.

A face is washed, shaved, teeth brushed, pants put on, shirts buttoned, shoes tied. A bald spot at the back of the head, bags under eyes, feet hurt.

A face is washed, teeth brushed, lipstick and eye liner added, a skirt pulled on, a blouse buttoned, shoes slipped on. Silver in hair that had no silver before, forehead wrinkled, a pelvis that ached since the baby.

It's like this.

A glass is raised. A bear dances. A man walks a Wolfhound down the street. A woman holds a man's head in her hands. A nurse takes a patient's blood pressure. A father knows where his daughter is. The music, guttural harsh.

It's like this.

He says no. He says yes.

He says nothing He says everything.

Night the Fourth

On his way down the corridor to see Elana, he saw her husband who glanced at him, hesitated for a moment, fixed him with a look.

He sees him with her at a café. He sees them walking in woods. He sees her raise a wine glass late at night. He sees him pull back the sheets. He does not see himself.

One night late he had driven Elana to his apartment. It was all right Elana said. He should not worry. He looked at her, thought of the car outside, waited to hear the engine. He imagined the husband look up at the windows in his apartment before he checked the rear view mirror, put the car into reverse, backed up, turned around in the driveway. He saw himself in the passenger seat alongside the husband.

Something must have happened. Anyone can visit during visiting hours at a hospital, but that did not mean Elana would let someone see someone he should not. She kept her worlds in order. There was the husband, friends, the friend more than a friend. One would nod to the other but the one who should not nod to him had just passed him going down the hall.

He was a friend. They read D. H. Lawrence, had seen *Annie Hall*. Everyone asked about him, but as weeks passed they wanted to know more. She was tired of it. As if they thought that

He did not know who would be the first to say it. Those who knew Elana, even those who did not, must have thought it at different moments, but had put it aside. There were reasons not to say anything. No one wanted to be the first to say what they did not want to hear.

All that had been put aside had come back when he passed the husband in the corridor. At the hospital. Where anyone could see them together. Anyone at all. A good friend. A very good friend.

Yes. But.

At midnight. The husband in Boston. Weekends walking in woods.

Please.

Holding hands in a café.

But.

Silence could no longer silence itself.

His mother never told anyone that he had been divorced. No one in the family had ever been divorced before. It was not just wrong, but failure. A moral failure. Marriage was a vow. You made your bed. You slept in it.

Mother could not bear the disgrace of it. At holidays she told everyone that his wife had to work. She could not make the trip west for the holidays. Her work was important.

She could not get her mouth around the word. She would not be able to live it down. Mother knew what the writing on the wall said, but would not look there. The word stuck in her throat and she could not spit it out.

Everyone knew he was divorced. The family never said what should be said but what was not said was how it got said.

He passed a nurse pushing a tiny, shrunken woman in a wheelchair down the hall. Wrinkles on her face deeply etched. Her hands twitched on her lap. A muscular kid with an earring and a tattoo on one arm followed behind them on crutches. A bald man with a pot belly his hospital gown did not conceal pushed an IV in front of him.

At the end of the hall they would turn around and see ahead of them what they had put behind them. The lives they had lived no longer lay ahead. Before was gone. After was left. An after that had no after after it.

He saw a tall blonde wearing a man's white shirt with the

cuffs rolled up, black tights. Her straw-blonde hair was tied behind in a pony-tail. She was here too. The woman he saw before Elana. As he entered Elana's room, he looked back. She was not there. She could not have been there. But it was a....

In a moment he would see his wife.

He looked at Elana, smiled. She did not disappear. He brushed her lips with a kiss, took her hand. Traffic had been heavy he said.

You saw him....

She could not help what happened. Her husband had to be in Boston tomorrow and she thought he would leave after work. He surprised her stopping at the hospital. She was pleased. She had not expected it. That he would....

Was he all right? She knew he was not comfortable around her husband. She tried to get him to leave. She smiled at him.

You know....

He was not unlike her husband. For a moment she ran a hand across her forehead, leaned back against the pillow.

Her husband carved figures out of stone, mostly birds. Once she suggested he do a sculpture of her. She laughed. He could not take his eyes off her. Of course he had seen her naked before, but all of a sudden he saw her as other men did.

He wanted to throw it away, but she wanted to keep it. It was not a very good likeness. She would show it to him sometime. It was not that he didn't see her as she was, but all of a sudden to see her as other men did rattled him. She ran a hand across her forehead, glanced at him. As her husband first saw her.

She first met him at an exhibit of her watercolors. She paused, examined her hands folded in her lap. In the city. She looked out the window. In another life.

She talked about his writing with her husband. That might be why she loved them. She could not love a man who went to work every day, went to work day after day without asking himself why he did. If there was not something more to life than work. For a moment she looked over his shoulder towards the hall.

A nurse wheeled a patient by but Elana continued to glance at what was now an empty hall.

She can do what she wants, but it was a small town. It was one thing for her to have coffee in a café with a man her husband said. It was another to go to his apartment. As long as she was discreet.

It was not that she had coffee with him or that she went to his apartment. But to spend time with a man who was not her kind. <u>This man</u>. He kept calling him that. <u>This man</u>. He did not understand what she saw in him. She took his hand, held it. Her husband would never understand.

Her husband put up with so much. In asking about him her husband was asking about himself. What kind of man was he? He understood about her first love. A first love is always at the door. But <u>This man</u>.

It's been….

She grimaced but when she saw the look on his face said he should not worry. Every day in the hospital is the same but some days the same is not the same. The nurse takes her blood pressure and frowns. She may have frowned yesterday but she did not notice it. Today she did. The nurse says. She's said it before, but today it is different.

Once she was hit by the car nothing was what it was before. She ran a hand across her forehead. For a moment she looked across the room, but he could not make out what she saw. In the hospital nothing is what it was before. At moments late at night she cries. She does not know why.

She does not cry because of how she feels or has had a sudden pain. She examined her hands. It just comes. With a finger she traced a vein on one hand. As if her body is telling her something she needs to hear.

She can't do anything herself. Nurses wash her, put a bed pan under her. She wants to get up, walk away, but can't, even if she could. She sat up, adjusted the pillow behind her head. He cannot know what it is like. She pulled the sleeve of her hospital gown up and rubbed an arm.

The doctor had stopped. He said she would be in the hospital a few days longer than they thought. The tibia and femur were not healing as fast as they thought they would.

He said….

She did not want to say anything more.

It's….

He should not worry. She did not want to talk about it. She paused, glanced at the ceiling before she looked back at him.

You….

She ran a hand across her forehead. She meant she. For a moment she looked at the pill containers, flowers friends had brought, a box of chocolates, the morning paper on the small table by the side of the bed.

A doctor and nurse hurried by in the corridor. An elderly couple stopped for a moment and looked in to see if this was the room they needed to visit. Elana bit her lip. Her eyes teared up. Somewhere there was a high-pitched cry that went on and on until suddenly it was cut off. She looked at him as if she had not seen him before.

She hears steps. She hears steps even when she knows she has not heard them. As if they are not anything human..

Steps hurrying somewhere, pausing, uncertain, slowing.

Steps at the end of a day, in the darkest hour of night, relentless.

Steps down the hall, fading.

She waits for a voice to ask if she is there. The slow intake of a breath, a sigh. He coughs, clears his throat. She does not want to know who it is. He will come into the room. He will say.

She does not want to know.

She looked away. As if something distracted her. Something that came to mind. A sound she could not place. She examined something she noticed on the bed. He could not see what it was.

She needs more books to read. He should bring her something cheerful, full of laughs. Not Dostoyevsky. She touched his hand, ran fingers down his arm. He always tells her she must read him, even if she has told him more than once she would not. Dostoyevsky was too bleak, obsessed by God, sin. She would not read Dostoyevsky.

Did he....

The day they walked by the swamp near the hospital. She can see the swamp through the window from her bed. They had seen so many birds. Wood thrushes, warblers, grackles, blue jays, a cardinal. Once they flushed purple finches. The sky slate-gray, overcast.

The hospital was nearby and she did not know it was there. She picked up a glass. For a moment she looked at him before she drank. Almond-shaped, Polish blue eyes. Limpid, wet. The hospital was nearby and she had not noticed it.

She had not understood that it was nearby so that she would be brought to it. As if that day the gods looked down and blessed them in order to take their blessing back. He'll think that's stupid. That the accident must have caused whiplash or something.

A week or two after he told Elana he could no longer be with her he called her. He just knew that when he heard her voice he would know what to say. When he heard her husky voice say hello, hello, excited, as if she were expecting the call, he could not say anything.

Her voice silenced him as if he understood for the first time that it was over. For a moment he said nothing. It's you, isn't it? Elana said at last. It's you. Her voice in his mouth. He waited a moment longer before he hung up.

He thought love would save him from the deadly labor of the every day, from whatever it was that dragged him down, kept him from.

It was not what he thought it would be. Now that it was gone she had brought him back. He did not know what would be next. All that he knew was he was here. He had to be.

Night the Fifth

She was asleep. Her face flushed, breath even. A whisper. Days she said she bit her lip. There were wrinkles on her forehead. Her face a mask.

No one can talk to her.

Life had become.

No one sees it. No one understands.

Night after night in the hospital she cried out in sleep, tossed, turned, grabbed blankets, pulled them up to her chin, pushed them aside. At moments her body suddenly became rigid. Pain she said that seized her like hands on her throat.

She did not take the pills she was given to relieve pain. Morphine she thought. She kept them to take when she got home to see what their effect on her would be. Did he remember the weekend he took her to see his friends? What it was like on the way home.

They knew they had seen themselves that night as they had not seen themselves before, but could not speak of it. On their way back from a weekend with friends of his, Elana gave him a marijuana brownie, took one for herself. She smiled, touched his hand. It was late. No traffic on the road. The sky dark. They passed freshly mowed fields, barns, silos.

The road lay ahead. The road always lay ahead he thought. Always an elsewhere to reach. Never a here that kept him. What was

Not what it had been before.

At one point Elana counted her fingers. There were ten of them she said. She counted them again. She was right. There were ten of them. She held up her hands to show him.

Later headlights of approaching cars were Fourth of July sparklers. Hubcaps diamonds. Tail lights blinked blood-red. They saw a shopping center, a factory, a gas station. All of a sudden the road veered right and he turned only to turn back abruptly when a corn field came rushing up.

For a moment he saw his grandparents working in a field somewhere in the high Tatras in Slovakia. They left the old country for the new world but could never escape the past. He saw himself in the field working behind them.

Look at the moon Elana said. The man in the moon. He

She pointed. It was him. The man in the moon. She grabbed his arm. The man in the moon.

They saw Elana's home on a street he did not recognize. As if it had been moved. As if one night had passed and the one that had come

They were downstairs.

A kaleidoscope of pulsing color.

They saw stairs.

One step waited for the next.

They were in the bedroom.

He recognized it.

In the hall a frail, elderly woman with a walker. A nurse at her side. The woman leaned on the walker, slid one foot forward, pushed the walker ahead, slid the other foot forward.

Time was all she had, even if for them that night time disappeared down the rabbit hole.

There was a man — or was it a woman? — on Elana's bed. He saw Elena on her knees in front of him. She was back, she said. She was home.

He remembers Elana rub her head against the man's thighs, touch his penis, take it in her mouth. When she raised up and kissed the man he could not turn away. There was a scratching sound of an animal behind him and he turned to see what it was.

When he looked back the man was no longer there. Elana beckoned him to her, shucked her levis off, slid panties down, spread her legs, touched herself.

Her fingers moving back and forth, at first slowly, lingering, then faster. For a moment she stopped, looked at him. Then she continued as if he were not there, one finger, then two, in and out, in and out.

He found himself kneeling between her legs. Her thighs warm, yielding, the dark, curly hair of her cunt wet against his tongue. She pulled the back of his head toward her.

A gale force wind rushed through him. High-pitched cries came from a place he did not know. His tongue frenzied, frantic.

Her thighs tightened around his head. She rocked back and forth. Suddenly he saw himself as she must see him and wanted to pull away. She thrust her sex against him and he heard her cry out a name. A name that was not his. He rolled away from her. His penis dribbled. The salty taste of her on his tongue.

He saw himself get up, turn away from her, leave the bedroom before he lost sight of himself.

The end of the hall in front of him.

The ceiling over his head.

The bedroom behind him.

He took a step.

The end of the hall far.

He looked up.

The ceiling high.

It will take time….

A doctor to a nurse, family, loved one. Family to whoever must hear. A loved one who must say what he does not want to say. He rubbed his eyes. His chest a taut band.

He had been someone else when he met her. She showed him who he was. It was no longer a shock that he was no longer what he once was but a shock that he once was what he once was.

He went back. Did she have vaseline? For a moment she

looked at him as if she knew who he was. A man like all men. A man like all men who take what is theirs.

He put her on her stomach, applied vaseline to the rosebud between the cheeks of her buttocks, inserted one finger slowly into her anus, then two.

He saw himself drive into her hard, as if he could not go into her far enough, her soft, elastic buttocks cushioning his penis, gripping him, pushing back. He grunted. She cried out. He bit her neck. She raked his thighs with her nails. If she

He did not care. He would open her up as she had not been opened before. For a moment he touched himself.

Afterward he felt bruised, as if it were not only his body that had taken a beating. He was someone he had not known before. He did not know who she was.

In the bathroom he shit as he had not shit before. He did not believe it was possible he had so much shit in him. When he got up at last, he had to sit down again. There was more. He was nothing but shit.

She lay on the bed, her back turned toward him. For a moment he touched the back of her neck before he pulled the sheet up. He found his clothes and dressed. She turned, looked at him.

He could not go. She could not be left alone. She took his hand. She needed him.

He had to go. He had to work. He pulled his hand away.

She looked at her hand which no longer held anything. Something she saw in it. Something that could not be anything other than what it was. Real in a way that it could not be dismissed.

She screamed. A cry not human. From deep in the ground, high in the sky above.

He had to dress her, hold her hand, guide her down the stairs, out the door and into the car. He had to drive. If a cop saw them.

He took the brake off, shifted gears, backed up, turned, put the clutch in, uncertain, tentative, as if he had not driven before.

A crow working on a flattened squirrel in the road flew up when they approached. A man walked his dog. A light went on in an apartment. A hand reached out a door to pick up a morning paper. Elana had not said anything. He did not know if she were awake.

He lay alongside her in his apartment, her head against his shoulder. He put an arm around her and pulled her close. She did not say anything. He did not know what to say. He saw himself pulling the covers over his head and turning away from her. He could not breathe.

The night sky lightened, gray becoming pale blue, streaks of pink, orange. He dressed, made himself coffee, stopped at the door, glanced at Elena.

He did not know why he did not call in sick. His father never did, even if he hated work, did just enough not to be fired and never enough to be promoted. His mother always worked. Even when she rested she had to do something. There was always something to do. He knew he would not call in sick. He made of work a fetish Elana said.

He does not look good….

A voice in the corridor. A voice in his head. A voice he always hears.

What happened surfaced from a part of themselves they did not know was there. It could not be taken back but they did not know what to do with it. It could not be left behind, but they did not want to bring it back.

One afternoon in a café she touched his hand, traced his fingers, the smooth, skin of his palm. There was a lump in one finger. A bruised knuckle.

Was there anything he would not do? She thought about it often. She had done things she thought she would never do. It was not a question of…

It had to do with...

For a moment she looked away before she held his hand in front of her face and examined it. She could not say what it was. She smiled at him.

It had to do with...

She knew he would not cross a line. She asked herself what he would be like if he did.

Did he….

It was a long night a nurse said. She'd bring him coffee. There were deeply etched lines across her forehead. She was pale. It must have been a long night for her.

Was he ok?….

He is here every night. He stays all night and goes to work the next day. She was not certain she would do it for her husband. She checked the IV, looked at the chart at the end of the bed. She shrugged. You do what you got to do. For a moment she looked at Elana. She touched his shoulder. Go she said. It's almost morning.

He nodded to her. In a moment. He glanced at Elana.

He sees her upturned nose rub against his shoulder. He feels a smile he cannot see. The tight muscles of his chest give way. The slow in and out, in and out of her breath. His pulse steady, sure.

He stretched his legs out in front of him, massaged his thighs. Go he tells himself. Walk down the hall and out the door. Day after day down a hall and out a door.

Night the Sixth

Last night….

It must have been a long night. He should have left. There was no reason he should have stayed. She was asleep. He had to go to work in the morning. She laughed. She must have been good company. After dinner....

For a moment Elana looked at a package in her hands. There were dark rings under her eyes. Her lips dry, cracked. Lines stretched across her neck. After dinner she....

Next thing she knew it was morning. Her glance remained on the package. She does not know why friends bring the gifts they do. They care. But.

They don't know what to bring. It's not as if it's a birthday or wedding. She ran a hand across her forehead. They tell themselves it does not matter. A present is a present.

She put the package aside, looked at him. She shouldn't be hard on them. They come. They bring presents. She smiled at him. It was good to see him.

But….

Friends come but can't stay. Nurses see other patients. She never sees some friends. She clasped and unclasped her hands in her lap.

Why….

It wasn't that. She traced a vein on the back of a hand, her glance intent on the movement of her finger.

Yesterday….

She hurt. She wanted to cry out. She squeezed his hand and brought it up to her cheek. She did.

She tried reading. She thought it might take her mind off how she felt but the words made no sense to her. She looked at him, as if she was not sure she should say anything more. For a moment she held his hand tightly before she let it go.

If she told herself a story she thought. Something to distract her.

In the watercolors she did, Elana drew dragons and devils, princes and princesses. Children in lands not of this world. There are places to go when we need to escape the world or ourselves but for Elana it had — always — to be one a child would seek out.

At first she imagined a prince and princess in a lovely castle on a hill. In the distance, a river beneath snow-covered mountains. A carriage approached the castle. She was in the carriage.

She clasped and unclasped her hands in her lap, looked out the window. There was a full moon overhead. Snow-covered fields behind the hospital glittered, luminous.

As if a remote control had been taken from her. Someone or something put on another channel.

It was….

She does not want to talk about it. She adjusted the sheet, moved the pillow behind her head. She drank water from a glass on the night table by the side of her bed. For a moment she held the glass in her hands.

She has to say something. It doesn't go away. When she turns to see if there is someone in the hall she sees men in suits in unmarked cars. When she hears a cry down the hall she sees women in the car in tight-fitting dresses and heels.

Headlights traced a path through darkness towards a chateau in woods. In a large hall in the chateau she saw men and women in masks. A naked woman was led in. A man held her head up to look at her more closely. A woman fondled a breast. A man told her to turn around.

Elana looked away. She brushed a lock of hair off her forehead. She bit her lip. She examined a stain on the sheet, ran a finger over it, rubbed it.

She saw a woman bent over a table. A man in a mask with

a whip. For a moment he rested the whip on her buttocks. Elana ran a hand across her forehead. A black leather belt on a woman's ass as if it lay on a table.

She thought she was the woman. In a moment she felt a hand touch her breast, caress a nipple. She waited for a hand to spread her cheeks. Her nipples hardened. The woman whispered something but she could not make out what it was. Then she did.

No. *yes.*

A yes that wrapped itself around her until she could no longer breathe. She cried out. A nurse came by and asked if she were all right. She glanced at the nurse. Was she all right? What did she mean? She was in a hospital. She had a broken leg.

Suddenly the nurse was no longer at her side but in the chateau alongside the other women. A woman who would be undressed, laid naked on a table, touched, probed, as she is in the hospital.

She glanced at a young man with flowers go by in the corridor. For a moment she continued to glance at the empty corridor after the man had gone by. She raised one hand up in front of her face and examined it.

She knows what he must think. She must have read *The Story of O.*, seen a movie on 42nd Street. She frowned. Women do not have to read the book. Every woman knows.

For a moment she looked at him before she looked away. Her lip quivered. She picked a glass up from the night table beside the bed, drank from it.

It was the hospital. One morning she wet herself. A nurse was by her side to clean her, as if she'd been waiting in the hall. The night they kissed. A nurse smiled when she came in. They know. They never miss anything.

They take her to surgery. Doctors and nurses wait as she saw them wait for the woman in the chateau. When she woke, she saw a nurse and doctor examine her eyes. They want her eyes too she thought. They would not stop until they had them. Until they had everything. For a moment she looked at him as if he might be one of them..

Would he move her back in bed? Just take her arms under the shoulders. As he leaned over her and put his arms under her shoulders, she touched his lips.

Tonight….

Look. Her eyes were open. She talked. She put a fixed smile on her face. A patient should be glad she has visitors. She felt so much better today. Ann brought a scrabble set. They could play.

She turned away so that he would not see her eyes tear up. She shredded kleenex. He got up, adjusted her pillow, rested a hand against the back of her head. She closed her eyes. Her breath fitful, cheeks red. She clutched the sheet.

In the hall he saw a man pause, look at him for a moment before he went by. A dean at the college. Fran did not say anything when he said he had to go to the hospital. She did not know what was going on but knew something was.

The Dean would not say anything, but it would not be him who said it. The days he had been seen with Elana at cafes or walking in fields. The nights he was at her home, Elana at his apartment. They knew that what they did had consequences but in the flush of what they had did not speak of them, if they even thought of them.

He sees himself in line waiting for a bus. It is dark. No one speaks. No one moves. A man turns up his collar. A man checks his watch. A woman closes her eyes. A man looks down the street. A woman shifts her bag to the other hand

It is Wednesday. It might be Monday, Friday. It is winter. Spring will follow, then summer, fall. It was like this yesterday, the week before, last month. It was like this last year and the year before. It will be like this next year. The factories wait. The office.

Elana was sorry. She closed her eyes to rest for a moment, but must have nodded off. She was not good company tonight. They should play scrabble. It would take her mind off....

It's....

When she woke in the hospital she did not know where she was. They told her she was in a hospital but it made no sense. As if she were back in Yugoslavia.

She was on her way to the library to see him. They had to talk.

Does he know what it is like? She was only crossing a street and found herself in a world she did not recognize. As if this is what it means to reach the other side. The other side we always come to.

He sees himself on the platform of a train station waiting for a train. A man touches his luggage with a foot. A woman wipes tears from her cheek. A man cups his hands to light a cigarette. A woman looks up at the station clock to check the time. She runs a hand across her forehead. It is morning, early morning. It might be night, late night. The train arrives at the same time in winter as it does in summer. The train leaves in spring as well as fall. The train takes them from where they are to where they are not. The train they must take. The train that waits for them.

Night the Seventh

It's....

A lie Elana says.

What the lie is she does not say. She does not want to talk about it. It's enough for him to know it is a lie.

It's....

Don't listen to what anyone says.

They believe what they want to believe. She glanced at him. He knows she will not lie to him. She swept a hand across the front of her body to take in....

Whatever needed to be taken in.

She has a husband. She goes to church. She pushed the greens of her salad around on the plate with a fork. The way they look at her. As if for her to be in church. She pushed the dinner tray away.

She is a New Yorker. They know what New Yorkers are like and make sure that she knows. Her voice exasperated, angry. They wrap their small town arrogance around themselves as if it is a scarf to keep out the cold. She could not get out what she had to say fast enough. There were beads of moisture on her forehead. They think they know everything. She put the fork down. They see only what they want to see. She bit off the words.

She looked at him, looked away. Her cheeks flushed, lips tightly closed. She pointed to something out the window but did not say what it was. She picked a book up from the night table beside the bed. She does not know why she is reading it.

It's....

For a moment she glanced at the paperback copy of *Wuthering Heights* in her hand. She can't figure out what bothers her about it. She must have read it before but does not remember she had. She took his hand. Her eyes glistening, bright.

She's….

It had been a difficult day. They put her in a wheelchair, explained to her what she should do. They gave her crutches, had her practice. Her arms are so sore. It was not easy. Several times she lost her balance. She lifted an arm and showed him red, raw skin under her arm.

When she's home she'll have therapy. She'll have to do exercises every day. On the street everyone will see her in a wheelchair or with crutches.

She's young. She's not a cripple.

She traced some lines on the sheet. They say she'll be what she was before, but that it will take time. She'll have to be patient. Her glance intent on the movement of her finger.

Her husband puts up with so much. When she goes home. She touched his thigh. Sometimes when she says something to him. She removed her hand, as if she should not have touched him.

It can be anything. Her husband looks at her without saying a word before he walks out of the room. When he comes back, he says she wants too much. She doesn't think of him. He works hard so that she can have the life she wants.

She raised a hand in front of her face, held up one finger, then a second. She looked at him, smiled. He did not know why.

He is always sorry. She gives him so much. How can he complain? He knows he blows his stack. At work they say

She shouldn't be talking about her husband. It's no one's business but hers. She would much rather talk about them. The afternoons they sat in a café or the library. For a moment she paused, glanced out the window, distractedly ran a hand over her cast.

We….

They would not have become lovers had they not talked for months. Their talk was real, as most talk is not. For a moment she paused. It had an urgency that did not rush past itself. As if what was said could be said only in the time of its time.

At some point he must have thought about sex. She took a kleenex from the end table. As if in some way their talk

It could not have been more intimate, close. It does not happen every day. Christ! Weeks may go by exhausted by the babble that washes over them.

As if their talk could complete itself only in bed. She laughed. She did remember that the first time it was the couch, not the bed. For a moment she examined the kleenex in her hand. Perhaps that's where all talk ends.

She knows men. She touched his thigh. When they say that she is beautiful. She rolled her eyes. When they say that she understands them as no one has. She saw him glance at her hand on his thigh. When they say she intimidates them. How is that possible? She is a woman.

He waited for what she would say next, but whatever it was she seemed to have forgotten it. She lay back against the pillow, closed her eyes. For a moment her lips moved but he could not make out what it was.

Her forehead wrinkled. She bit her lip. She turned away from him. In a moment turned back, her mouth open, breath uneven. Her fingers tugged at the blanket.

What....

She did not remember what it was. In the hospital she falls asleep before she finishes a sentence. Someone says something but she can't remember what it was.

Doctors say she should not have sex her first weeks at home. She ran a hand across her forehead. Her leg was not fully healed. She touched him.

She can't help it. The longer she is here the more she thinks about sex. For a moment she traced lines on the sheet. It is the only thing she thinks about. As if she were talking to herself. She counted the lines she has made.

It was the hospital. Its endless examination of the body. Its relentless attention to bodily functions.

It was the accident. The pain at moments so intense she cannot stand it. She pulled the sheet up.

She remembered the best sex she's had to take her mind off the pain..

The man. Men. A woman. A threesome.

She counted up the places she's had sex.

A hotel room. The woods. The back seat of a car. A library.

It may not always have been the best time but whenever it happened it was the right time.

She tells herself she must do everything before it is too late. In the camps people had sex before they were sent to the gas chambers.

She lay back, examined the ceiling. She looked at him, looked away, blew her nose with kleenex, balled the kleenex up, dropped it on the bed. She picked up another kleenex, shredded it.

She sees herself tied up and whipped. She glanced at him. The books women read that give them. She waved a hand back and forth in front of her.

Whatever they need. Whatever they did not know they needed. The not having it that sends them to other men or women. That sends them to the therapist. She laughed. By the time they see the minister, they can no longer be saved.

Would he give her the glass of water? After she drank she held the glass in her hand for a moment. When no one comes to see her. She pointed to the tv. She won't watch it.

She waits for someone. Anyone. When a nurse comes in to take her blood pressure

It is only a nurse. She has to do what she does. But when she sees her at the door, it is like. Her hands held tightly together in her lap. It is like.

As if it she had been rescued.

At the end of her life her grandmother talked about how she met grandfather. The day they went to the lake and afterwards went to a café. Grandma would never forget what granddad said, how he held her hand.

This morning she remembered the first time she put on lipstick, when she had her first period, the first boy she went out with who did not call back. Her first love. After he left her.

Her life is not over as her grandma's was when she remembered what it was like when she met grandpa. She put a hand to her forehead. But.

Whatever she had said or done before is different now. She plays the game we all play, nods when she is to nod, says yes when she should say yes, the buts, you knows, if it were not fors, nos, you're rights we live by. But when she hears herself now.

Does he ever hear himself? No one should hear himself. If they ask her one more time how she feels, she'll scream. She wants to throw food.

She's sorry. With the back of her hand she wiped mucus from her nose. Soon she'll be home. She ran a hand across her forehead. She wants to see him. She'd missed him horribly.

She doesn't understand why he ended it. The day she was hit by the car she had been on her way to the library to see him. She had to talk to him.

He remembered a day he had come home and seen a couple he did not know in the living room. In the kitchen, his wife introduced him to a man at her office. She put an arm around his shoulder. She did not know what she would do without this man. As if a door had been opened into a room in which he did not belong.

It was not that he was difficult. That he would shrug his shoulders and not say anything as if his silence said all there was to say. That he would drink too much and examine the bottom of the glass as if it would tell him who he was.

He could not cross the streets he had to cross to make his way in the world. Wherever he was was not where he should be. Whatever he was a stranger to himself.

He did not say anything. Elana would see him when she would. He would want to see her more. She would make the effort. It would not be enough. There would be the weekend she saw. The night someone came by. She would make it up to him. Not now. Later. There would always be later. He brushed strands of hair off Elana's forehead, took her hand.

Night the Eighth

He should not be here. Her mother-in-law called and said she would be in town, would stop at the hospital. She pushed her head back against the pillow. She tried to call him. Why was he here when he should not be?

She can no longer keep anything straight. Everything that has happened. That goes on. She has a fever. When someone says something she does not always understand what they say. Where the voice had come from. The cast on her leg makes her skin itch until she has to scratch it. Sometimes she can't stop until it is raw.

She brushed hair off her forehead. For a moment she looked at him in a way he did not understand. Her forehead wet with perspiration. Strands of hair pasted against it.

They were not getting any younger her husband says. They had done what they wanted to do, gone where they wanted to go, lived as they had. What had happened made him think if. It could have been worse. Much worse. It was time they should settle down, think about a child, a family. High time he said. God! High time.

He said. He said. He said….

She wanted to scream. She'd been hit by a car. She was in a hospital. She did not want to think about children. Why bring them up now? She turned away, rubbed her nose against the pillow, one hand clasped into a fist over the edge of the bed.

There were times he had not used a condom with Elana. In a field one day. The back seat of a car. She disliked condoms and could have become pregnant, but no one, not even Elana, would know who the father was.

His wife had been pregnant. It had not been planned. They had not talked about children. There was no discussion. She would not be a mother. He did not ask himself why his wife was pregnant. She was on the pill. He did not want to think about it.

Elana was not certain she'd ever be the same. The doctor said she might have a slight limp. It depended on rehab. Even then

The doctor did not say what. She should not worry. They would talk about it if need be.

She thought of Yugoslavia. When she slit her wrists in college. The sliver of glass embedded in her hand from a childhood accident.

In the hall, a man leaned on crutches. His face red, wet. His glance on something ahead of him.

Whenever she hears an ambulance she knows it is coming for her..

She glanced at him. Polish blue eyes as deep as a midwest sky on cloudless August days. Polish blue eyes wherever he goes. Polish blue eyes waiting for him to turn around.

As if every night he is a priest at confessional. She can hold nothing back. How does he listen to this shit? She would have left and not come back. For a moment she looked at him as if she understood something about him she had not known before.

A nurse had come up to the man with crutches. In a moment she took his arm and led him down the hall.

She does not want to think of a child, but when she has one, she knows it will be a girl.

The skin of her cheeks and forehead stretched, tight. At moments she would run a hand over her face to smooth whatever lines she thought were there.

Perhaps she should. To think of herself holding a girl, bathing her, talking to her. What it would be like to have a girl at her breast. For a moment she traced a vein across the back of a hand. It would take her mind away from how she feels.

She was always saying that, wasn't she? Would he get her a glass of water? If it is not one thing, it is another. She waved a hand back and forth in front of her as if to take in where she is, what happened.

After she drank she held the glass in her hand, her glance fixed on it.

She was in bed.

She was in a hospital.

She held a glass.

Who, where and when were clear, but what had become increasingly uncertain if not ambiguous. Why had no answer. The glass held her.

Not that anything happens. In the hospital nothing changes. The nurse comes by, takes her blood pressure, gives her medicine, checks her leg, looks at the chart. Then it is the doctor's turn. She can tell the time of day from who is there.

In the distance the faint whistle of a train. The tracks were alongside the river downhill from the hospital. Every day at three she heard a train. Every night late, well after midnight, as he knew, there was another. Why they heard a train now. This early in the evening

She ran a finger around the rim of the glass, her glance intent on the movement of her finger. Her lips moved as if she said something.

This afternoon....

She put herself in the wheelchair. She needed to know how to use it. At first she was afraid she could not. That she would do something she could not control. The chair get away from her. But once she got used to it. To what it could do. What it did. What she could do. Needed to do. Did. She ran a hand across her forehead.

She went by rooms in which patients were asleep, watched tv, read, talked to loved ones. She went by rooms in which patients stared dumbly at the ceiling as if the ceiling had answers. She went by nurses, a doctor, one patient with an IV.

At one room a man gestured to her. He had tubes in his nose. An IV dripped into one arm. She could not guess how old he was, but you knew he was old.

She pushed herself into his room. He must need something she thought. A nurse had not come.

He did not say anything. She did not know if he could. He looked at her but did not seem to see that anyone was there. Then he saw her.

She would not forget that look. No woman does.

She could....

He needed it. Why should she not? What could anyone do? He could not even raise his head, but when she touched him he became hard. She stroked him. His eyes were closed. His breath heavy, choked.

If she'd been seen. What she did was dangerous. They would say she was sick. A pervert.

For a moment something on the bed caught her attention She ran a hand across the blanket, picked up what looked like a thread, examined it for a moment, let it go.

She hates them. What she did was right but they would say she was a pervert. The man needed what she gave him. What was the wrong? What she did was good for him. They have no compassion. Her tone bitter.

She smiled. As if the thought of them. Good citizens she dismissed more than once. Chamber of Commerce church-goers. Uptight, repressed. Those who do not live because for them to live is wrong. The tip of her tongue pressed against her lip.

It was good for her. It did more for her than the doctors have. She cannot describe what it was like. The smile on his face after he came.

The man would not say anything. Not that Elana made

him hard when he may have thought it was no longer possible. That someone cared when he thought no one any longer did. He was not alone. One did not speak about deliverance.

Today....

So much happened. It was hard to take it all in. She ran a hand across her forehead. Her mother-in-law will be here soon. She does not want to think about how she'll have to be when she is. It's not that she does not like her. She is a nice woman, but her idea of nice....

She would not like some of what she has done, if she were to know.

She will nod, smile to her, say yes, she's better. She has a good doctor. The nurses are there when she needs them. Yes. She misses her husband. Friends have come by.

For a moment she pasted a smile on her face before she wiped it off. She began to trace some lines on the blanket.

You become what everyone wants you to be. You get used to being what you cannot escape.

In a low voice, barely a whisper.

He did not want to be here when her mother-in-law arrived any more than Elana did. He would smile, nod, say yes. He would laugh. A laugh more hollow than anyone will know. He rubbed his eyes. An overwhelming weariness overcame him.

He should go...

He had come to the hospital he told himself because he was doing what any friends of hers would do. The friend he knew that some thought more than a friend. Nurses, like waitresses or bartenders, know what everyone does not tell their families, priests or analysts. Every night Scheherazade sits at their side.

Nothing was what it was. Nothing is ever what it is. He was here because he had left. He had come back because he had not gone. She would not let him breathe.

If he would wheel her to the end of the hall. She can point out the room where the man was. She will kiss him good-bye. It's been so long.

It's better that he not meet her mother-in-law. She would ask about him.

Night the Ninth

She's….

There were moments she did not think that she would get better. When they said her leg was healing slowly. When they told her the rehab she would have to do. When they

It would not happen. She knew it would not happen. She would not get better. But she is going home. Does he believe it? She's not sure she can.

She's….

relieved. So relieved. She'd put lipstick on, dark eye liner. Someone had pinned a rose to her hospital gown. Her eyes large in her head. Suddenly she laughed. She cannot believe it.

There had been so many days in the hospital she felt she would not recover. Whatever she had done before, whatever it had been, some mistake, something that had gone wrong, some loss she suffered had not set her back as much as this had. No one can know what is was like.

A nurse came in with a bouquet of spring flowers from her husband. Elana put them up against her face, took in their fragrance. She was pleased Elana was going home. It had not been easy for her. For a moment the nurse glanced at him.

Every day he is at her side. Every day he asks himself why he is. He had ended it. But what was over was less clear. The call from the hospital called him on it. You think you can escape but you never do.

These nights brought them closer together. There were couples who did not have what they had, who did not know if they had anything, who knew it was gone. But when she smiled at him. When she took his hand.

What did he not understand? He could have stayed with her on her terms, but when you end up in the emergency room and they find nothing wrong with you, something is wrong. He had ended it not out of any understanding of what an end might be but to stop an anguish that could not be stopped.

What did he not understand? Her hand on his. A smile that knew him like no one else. A light in her eyes that lit a road he had not been down before.

Yesterday Elana used the wheelchair. Today she used crutches. Tomorrow her husband would wheel her down the hall, out the door and back into her life.

He should say something but did not know what to say, would not know how to say it, even if he did. There was too much to say and too little that could be said. The excluded middle between the not enough and the too much defied him.

For them to live they had to lie. They had to lie not to lie.

That she was going home. That. At last. She can think of nothing else. There were moments she thought it would never happen. When she was in the wheelchair yesterday, she did not think. It was so sudden.

Come here….

Life will be like what it was before, even if it will be different. She'd been hit by a car. She'd been in a hospital. She laughed. She wants to take him home with her. She took his hand.

You're….

She was sorry. She was so excited that she was going home that she did not give him a chance to say anything. Think of what it will be like. They can meet in cafes as they did in the past. He'll be able to sleep nights. She smiled. He should not be so sure.

The time they walked and talked, stopped to look at, see, saw in the nature trail outside the town. Before they realized it, they were on the ground and he was entering her when a group of workers going down a trail to clear it saw them and high-fived them. Elana was delighted.

This might be better than she thought it would be. When she wheels herself down the street everyone will stop and ask her what happened. Those who do not know her, have no idea who she is.

The woman seen in church Sundays, at lectures at the public library or concerts at the college who always made sure that she determined how she was seen.

He did not like the man who would not let her live her life but would force her to live his. The man he despised in other men. The man he was. Who would remain who he was because he could be no one other than himself.

He sees himself in his apartment reading on the black leather couch. For a moment he looks up at the Victorian rocker his ex-wife refinished, at a photograph of a window of an apartment in Florence with flowers in it, at an oval mirror that a love bought him.

— *Can he believe it?...*

He sees himself get up, put Coltrane's *A Love Supreme* on, go into the kitchen to boil water for coffee. While the water boils, he sees birds at the feeder outside the window.

She's going home....

He takes his coffee into the study, picks up Melville's *Pierre*, glances at it for a moment, reads several pages at random. The love of Pierre for two women, neither of whom he can have. On the wall there is a Munch print, a copy of a Tina Modotti photo. For a moment he runs a hand over the keyboard of the typewriter on the desk.

Alone.

She...

We do what we can. We do what we can and it is never enough.

When she called him from the hospital, she knew he would answer. He had done what he'd been asked to do — done what he wanted to do — but now it was impossible to go back, pick up where they had left off three months ago, as if he had been on a trip and was glad to be home.

Cobalt blue, almond-shaped eyes, flecked with gold on him. Polish blue eyes. Sharply-angled Slavic cheeks. The tip of a tongue pressed against an upper lip. For a moment he turned away from her.

The hall empty. Someone would come by. Someone would leave. He sees her husband. He sees one of her lovers. He does not see himself. Not that he has left. Just that when he was there he never saw himself.

When she called him he said he was glad she did. To be with her in the hospital. But now. She was going home. Her life would go on as it had. He would no longer see her.

He had said what he did not want to say but it was the only thing he could say. He could not do it before. He cannot do it now. The utopia of an existence that would be free of the burden of being himself could not be his.

For a moment she looked at him as if she had not heard what he said. Her lip trembled. She raised a hand in front of her as if to ward him off. She screamed. A hoarse animal cry, not a sob but savage, an attack, outrage, disbelief and refusal against anything that had held her back, an illness she had done nothing but live, as if it were life itself, years of darkness loving and being loved by men reaching every corner of the room, into the corridor, down the hall, out the door, into the night.

Six Months Later

The sky cloudless, pale blue, azure. There was no wind. Workmen were at work on the grounds, trimming bushes, cutting a lawn. A few minutes before the end of the hour. In the distance, a squirrel raised itself on its hind legs, as if it heard something. The only sound that of the phone. Elana Fran says.

They did not have to say anything because it had already been said. The time they had seen one another after she left the hospital went where it did because they knew it would not go anywhere. She would not leave her husband for a man she could not live with. He would love a woman who could not be his. What they understood — what they had — was enough.

Weekends in Montreal and New York that were joyous if calm, understanding that these might be last times because they knew at some point that they would be. Then they knew that they were. Elana's husband had been transferred to Boston. She was pregnant. She would be a mother.

Outside a jay perched on a branch of a tree. A squirrel motionless with a nut in a paw. Summer break and no students around. A faculty he knew walked across the quad to his office.

Lunch....

Fran looked up from the manuscript she examined. There was nothing on the calendar. The in-box had nothing pressing. Not much happened in summer. It might be a long lunch she thought.

He remembers the first time they made love he had come out of the bathroom afterwards and not knowing what he would say said that this was not playing, he wanted them to risk something, that there was too much compromise in life, too much sacrifice of desire to comfort and he was sick of it. She sat on a chair with one leg lifted, her foot on the seat, her chin resting on a knee, and looked at him in a way he did not understand.

She's leaving. Boston….

Polish blue eyes looking into his: here, now.

ACKNOWLEDGMENTS

In the first section of this novel there are a few unacknowledged quotations in the text:

Page 6: "Whether she wants it to or not her finger starts to move, her wrist bends, her hand presses down, her dance begins." Unica Zurn, *The Man of Jasmine*, 95.

Page 51: "How is she to find her way back to life if the dream never ceases to invite her to join the dance? Slightly modified. Zurn, *The House of Illnesses*, 39

Page 57: "When she talks into silence she doesn't know where her words come from." Slightly modified. Zina Trotsky in Ken McMullen's film, *Zina*.

Page 59: "She has to say what she has to say, what she has been unable to say, and when it is said, when she has buried every word that cannot be said." Slightly modified. Emily Holmes Coleman, *The Shutter of Snow*, 4.

Page 61: "Someone traveled inside me, crossing from one side to the other." *The Man of Jasmine*, 26.

Page 115: "Waiting for what happened to happen." Maurice Blanchot, *Awaiting Oblivion*, 85.

Robert Buckeye is author of four previous works of fiction about Puerto Rico (*Pressure Drop*), the Kent State shootings (*Still Lives*), Edvard Munch (*The Munch Case*) and Bratislava (*Fade*) as well as a study of the English novelist, Ann Quin (*Re: Quin*). In 2015, Spuyten Duyvil published a collection of his criticism, *Living In.* He divides his time between Vermont and Bratislava.